A Tangled Web

STAR WARS

THE LAST OF THE JEDI

A TANGLED WEB

Jude Watson

SCHOLASTIC INC.

New York   Toronto   London   Auckland   Sydney
Mexico City   New Delhi   Hong Kong   Buenos Aires

www.starwars.com
www.scholastic.com

No part of this publication may be reproduced in whole or in part, stored in a retrieval system, or transmitted in any form or by any means, electronic, mechanical, photocopying, recording, or otherwise, without written permission of the publisher. For information regarding permission, write to Permissions Department, Scholastic Inc., 557 Broadway, New York, NY 10012.

ISBN-13:978-0-439-68138-4
ISBN-10:0-439-68138-3

12 11 10 9 8 7 6 5 4 3   6 7 8 9 0 1/0

Printed in the U.S.A.
First printing, August 2006

STAR WARS

THE LAST OF THE JEDI

A Tangled Web

CHAPTER ONE

He hadn't seen Palpatine since he was seventeen. Ferus Olin remembered a pale, soft-spoken man with a sharp political mind. Chancellor Palpatine always had an air of deference to all, despite his considerable power in the Senate.

But things had changed.

He was the Emperor now . . . and his power had turned sinister.

Ferus was shocked. Palpatine's face had sunken into itself, his cheeks collapsed, his eyes hollowed. He wore a concealing hood, but it couldn't hide his newly grotesque appearance. The whites of his eyes had turned yellow, and his skin was deeply furrowed.

No wonder he no longer appeared on the HoloNet for official pronouncements.

Obi-Wan Kenobi had told him that Palpatine was a Sith. That he had fought in a battle with Mace Windu and had defeated him, but the effort of it had left him horribly scarred. Ferus hadn't known what to expect, but this was worse than he could have possibly imagined. He could feel the dark side of the Force in the room. He had to fight to keep his concentration.

Palpatine's aides, Sly Moore and Mas Amedda, stood at both ends of his desk. His Royal Red Guards — six of them — stood at attention near the exit door. A thin graying man with sunken cheeks, dressed in an Imperial uniform, stood near them. Ferus had no idea who he was, but the way he stood spoke of a certain importance.

All this, Ferus thought, *for little old me?*

Palpatine had contacted him only a few days before. He had asked him to this meeting, even though Ferus had recently escaped from an Imperial prison. The Emperor had guaranteed his safety. When Ferus had arrived, he'd undergone a standard weapons check, but to his surprise, Sly Moore had allowed him to keep the lightsaber he had clipped to his utility belt. He hadn't bothered to hide it. He knew Palaptine was aware that he had one.

"Please sit," Palpatine said, gesturing to a chair. "Make yourself comfortable. You see we allowed you to keep your weapon. A lightsaber . . . how interesting. And here I thought you were a *former* Jedi."

"Former apprentice, actually."

Palpatine sat and folded his hands on his desk. Ferus wrenched his eyes away from the Sith's long, deeply furrowed nails, caked with dirt. "I could hardly expect you to admit to being a Jedi, seeing that they were traitors who tried to bring down the Republic."

"I'm confused," Ferus said. "I thought it was *you* who brought down the Republic. Didn't you declare an Empire a couple of months ago?"

"I'm curious as to how you obtained a lightsaber," Palpatine said, ignoring Ferus's question. "Strange to see, because we received reports that a ship had landed on Illum, where so many lightsabers are created."

"Did you? I'm glad to hear it's still a popular place."

Palpatine gave a thin smile. "Only for the Jedi, and they are all gone now."

"I heard that, too."

"It was a shame that such a respected order overstepped its bounds so badly."

"Is that what happened? I had no idea."

Ferus felt sweat bead up on his hairline and hoped the Emperor wouldn't see it. He was feeling Palpatine out, trying to provoke him. But Palpatine just continued to speak in the same deep, sonorous voice, close to expressionless.

"Perhaps now we should discuss why I asked you here," the Emperor said.

"I have to admit I'm curious," Ferus said.

He had debated whether to come. He had been on a remote space station with his crew when the summons came. They were a scruffy bunch, made up of members of a group called the Erased, which included Keets Freely, a former journalist, and Curran Caladian, who had been a Senate aide. Also along was Clive Flax, who had escaped from the same prison as Ferus. Ferus was fond of Clive, who had been a double agent during the Clone Wars but claimed to owe allegiance to no one but himself. And then there was Trever, the street kid who'd been traveling with Ferus. Trever had been a stowaway on his flight from his homeworld of Bellassa, and the two had journeyed together ever since.

Also along was Solace, a reluctant traveler. She'd once been the great Jedi Knight Fy-Tor-Ana. She'd changed her name and had tried to forget her past existence as a Jedi. So she hadn't been too thrilled when Ferus came along, suggesting she team up to find other missing Jedi.

They'd been on their way to the secret base Ferus had set up for any Jedi he might find, when the summons had come from Palpatine. Ferus had been trying to get back there for weeks now. He needed to know how Jedi Master Garen Muln was faring.

Ferus had found him in the caves of Illum, waiting for death to take him. He'd still been weak when Ferus had left him in the care of his friends, Raina and Toma.

The Erased had all conferred, argued, and then, in the end, decided that Ferus couldn't ignore the summons. Besides, they reasoned, he might learn things from Palpatine that could be useful in the coming fight against him.

It was too dangerous for his friends to be near the Senate. They had gone to the secret hideout of Dexter Jettster, hundreds of levels below on Coruscant. If Ferus didn't return that day, they would come looking for him.

The thing was, he'd just had a hard time breaking out of an Imperial prison. He didn't want to end up in one again.

"I don't break my promises," Palpatine said. "You will be allowed to leave once you hear my proposal. I'm hoping you will accept it, but if not, the door will be open. However, I have no doubt you *will* accept."

Think again. There was no way Ferus would help the Empire. But for the moment, he'd keep his mouth shut.

"I'll let you be briefed by Moff Tarkin, who has been in constant contact with our Imperial advisor on Sath."

The tall man with the gray skin and dark hair took one step forward.

"We have received a request from a planet called Samaria through our own Imperial advisor there," he said. "The Samarian ruler has asked us to send an emissary directly from this office to help them. Their mainframe computer for the city systems of the capital city of Sath has been infiltrated. A bug has been introduced into the system that has transferred personal information from one citizen to another in a random pattern — and thus has thrown the banking, medical, and social services into chaos. Not only that, but the city systems have also malfunctioned. Do you know Samaria?"

"I've heard of it," Ferus said. "Never been there. I do know it's a desert planet, completely dependent on technology. I would imagine that this problem would eventually lead to major systemic breakdowns."

"Excellent," Palpatine said. "You have the picture entirely. Already, there is danger that the planet will collapse into anarchy."

Tarkin continued in the same terse tone. "The bug has been introduced so cleverly that no one can figure out how to kill it. Every time they've tried to fix it, it sends the programs into another random sequence. If the planet has to start over and collect information on every citizen, it could be disastrous."

Tarkin stepped back, his moment in the spotlight over. He seemed such a colorless presence . . . yet Ferus's instincts told him to beware.

"You can see why I've come to you, Master Olin," Palpatine said. "Since you've popped up, I've had occasion to read your file. You have an impressive history since leaving the Jedi. You're the best in the galaxy at computer security."

"I wouldn't say the best."

"I would."

In a former life, Ferus had been an expert at computer systems and identity coding. His company, Olin/Lands, had helped people disappear into new lives and had been expert at security wipes and the creation of new ID docs.

He could guess how much trouble the planet of Samaria was in. But that didn't mean he'd be an agent of the Empire.

"You were the most proficient in the galaxy," Palpatine continued. "No one else has been able to solve this problem. Your job will be to trace the saboteur through the system and find the key that will lead you to who did this. Then the Empire can restore the planet to stability. After all, stability is why the Empire began. We will reign over an unparalleled number of peaceful years. And we will always reach out a hand to help any planet in distress."

And if you believe that, you'll believe any-thing.

"I appreciate your problem," Ferus said. "Unfor-tunately, I can't help you."

Under the hood, the dark gaze flickered.

"I'm needed elsewhere," Ferus continued. "Now, since you assured me your exit door was open, I'll take my leave."

"If you must. Let him go," Palpatine instructed the Royal Guards.

Ferus walked toward the door. He waited at any moment for the Guards to strike him down on Palpatine's order. He wouldn't hesitate to use his lightsaber. If he had to die here, he would. There was no way he was going back to prison.

"There is just one more thing you should con-sider," Palpatine said.

Ferus stopped, his eyes on the door — and freedom. Here it was. He must have been a fool to think for even a second that Palpatine would let him go.

"You probably haven't heard the news. Your partner, Roan Lands, has been arrested."

Ferus felt the name like a stab in his heart. His partner. His friend. Roan.

Still, he kept his face to the door. He wouldn't give Palpatine the satisfaction of seeing his face.

"Along with an acquaintance of yours, Dona Telamark."

Dona, who'd hidden him when the Imperial soldiers were hunting him. Who'd asked for nothing and had given him everything. She was an elder woman, strong and sturdy, who loved her mountain home and her solitude. The thought of her in a prison was wrenching.

"They are both," Palpatine said, his voice rising, "scheduled to be executed."

Ferus tried not to shake.

"For what crime?" he asked.

"Conspiracy against the government of Bellassa."

What a joke. The government of Bellassa was under the domination of the Empire. Nobody would be foolish enough to conspire against it.

Palpatine's voice curled around his ear, thick and rancid. "However, if you could extricate yourself from your other commitments, I could request leniency from the Bellassan government. Perhaps even clemency."

There it was — the catch.

Just like that. Snap. He was caught.

He'd expected a catch. He just hadn't expected it to be so personal.

CHAPTER TWO

Trapped.

He'd walked right into it.

He'd had to agree to Palpatine's request. He'd had no choice.

Furious, he strode down the hallway that connected him to the main Senate building. He couldn't believe he had just agreed to work for a Sith.

He felt disgusted with himself, but he saw no way out — not if Roan and Dona's lives were on the line. Now he was headed to the Senate landing platform, where Palpatine had arranged a starship for him.

The usual crowd of senatorial aides, assistants, droids, and Senators swirled all around him. BD-3000 luxury droids hovered near the Senators, oozing compliments into ears and fluffing up capes. It was a sight he remembered well from his years on Coruscant.

Yet he did not feel the same sense of busy discord

he remembered from earlier times. Once there had been the buzz of conversations and arguments. Now there were blocs of Senators walking in lock-step, their rich robes in bright colors. Their collars, the larger the better, were made of fur or stiff silk and framed their glossy, well-fed faces. They were followed by trails of assistants, dressed just a shade less extravagantly than their bosses. Ferus saw more displays of wealth, and less displays of deference. There did not seem to be the busy hum of important work being discussed.

The Senate had changed, and he wanted no part of it.

A new addition to the Senate was the constant presence of Prowler 1000 seeker droids. They could be assigned to track any individual. He was certain that from the minute he stepped foot out-side Palpatine's office, his movements were being watched.

He'd have no opportunity to get to Dex's hideout now. He couldn't even risk using his comlink. He had to assume that comm transmissions were moni-tored. Somehow he'd have to find a way once he was on Samaria. He couldn't trust the comm unit on the ship, either.

Trapped.

Ahead he saw a worker mopping up the hallway. Dressed in bright yellow coveralls, the man bent over the vibromop, putting as little energy as possible into the task. His dark hair was covered by a rag that he had knotted in four corners, and he wore a face mask, no doubt to protect his lungs from constantly breathing in the strong cleanser. He swung the vibromop wide, and Ferus had to dance away in order to prevent himself from tripping over it.

"Sorry about that, mate," the worker said, and Ferus realized with a pleased shock that it was Clive.

"I see you've found your calling at last," Ferus murmured. He bent down to pretend to examine a spray of cleanser that had dotted his trousers. "They've arrested Roan and Dona."

The prowler buzzed overhead, and he moved on. Within a few steps he saw a cafe, one of the many eating areas tucked underneath the overhangs on the Senate's main hallways. A waiter was sponging off a table, dressed in the gray tunic the servers wore. Now that he was alert for it, Ferus picked out Keets right away.

He stopped at the counter and ordered a small cup of juice. He stood, sipping it, as the line moved forward, shielding him momentarily from the prowler. Keets approached to wring out the sponge at the sink near Ferus.

"Heading directly to Samaria," Ferus said as he turned away.

He walked down the hallway, turned the corner,

and saw a young boy selling the *Senatorial Record Digest.* Although the Senate cam droids sent official transcripts directly to the computers of the Senators, many of them still preferred to pick up durasheet copies of the digest, which summarized the events of a day, hour by hour.

This time, the newsboy was Trever, his bluish hair covered by a cap with a visor that shadowed his face.

Ferus reached out for the newssheet. "Blackmailed me to take the job," he said, tossing Trever a credit.

He pretended to scan the *Record* as he walked, then tossed it in a wastebin by a fresher. He waved his hand over the sensor to enter. The prowler followed him inside. The droid was as impossible to shake off as bantha drool.

He paused to wash his hands. An attendant handed him a towel. It was Oryon, his Bothan friend. Oryon had swathed his powerful frame in coveralls and his luxuriant mane in a close-fitting cap.

He dried his hands. "Computer systems crash on Samaria," he murmured.

He walked out. He knew that they would pass each tidbit of information along until they had a full picture of his dilemma. Despite his predicament, his heart felt full. He was surrounded by friends. Each one of them was wanted by the Empire. Each one of them was endangered by being here. Yet they were here.

Ferus reached the landing platform. He saw a pilot drinking a mug of tea by the opulent personal transports of the Senators. He was a slender Svrenini in a pilot's uniform. It was Curran Caladian, his furred face neatly combed, his bright eyes covered by the visor on his helmet. Ferus walked by him, pretending to admire a gleaming Nubian yacht with a chromium hull.

Drawing closer, he said, "I'll be going to the city of Sath. Reporting to an Imperial advisor."

He walked on. The only one of his crew he hadn't seen was Solace, but he didn't expect to. Out of all his friends, she was the most wanted by the Empire. The entire Imperial army and security forces, as well as Coruscant police, were on the alert for her. She had fought a battle in the underworld of Coruscant, trying to protect the group she'd gathered in the caverns of the underground oceans. She'd personally taken down squads of stormtroopers. It was truly too dangerous for her to be here.

An Imperial officer met him at the ship and told him the coordinates were already entered into the nav computer. The ship would need no refueling. He was not to stop at any space station. They were awaiting him in Sath. He was to land directly on the prime minister's landing platform.

The officer turned away as Ferus started toward the ramp. Suddenly another pilot accosted him.

"Don't think you're jumping the fueling line, fella," she said in a grating tone. "I've been here for twenty minutes."

It was Solace. She had disguised herself so well he didn't think he'd have been able to pick her out if she hadn't said something. She seemed taller and broader. She wore a black helmet and gloves up to her elbows, and tall boots.

"Got all the info," she told him quickly. "I'll take Trever and Oryon to Bellassa to track Roan and Dona. Trever knows the ropes there. Keets and Curran will stay on Coruscant and dig for information. Clive will follow you to Samaria."

Her calm dark eyes met his for a moment. "I will find Roan and Dona. I'll bring them to safety."

It was a promise, from one Jedi to another.

They didn't say it, but their gazes sent the message: *May the Force be with you.*

Ferus turned and strode up the ramp. Moments later, the ship shot out into the space lanes. He headed for the hyperdrive ring, and he was off.

CHAPTER THREE

Samaria was a small planet in the tiny system of Leemurtoo, in a strategic area of the Core Worlds. After receiving permission to land, Ferus buzzed over the city of Sath to get an airborne view.

The Samarians had manufactured a huge bay that was channeled into large canals that ran though the city. Along the edges of the bay, the engineers had built fingers of white sand that flung out into the aquamarine water, forming flowerlike designs. On these fingers were the most exclusive buildings, primarily residences and offices for the rich. The buildings were topped with domes that competed for attention, each with its own rich color and metallic inlays.

The complex of buildings that comprised the royal court of Samaria took up one whole flower made up of ten long petals with gleaming white buildings built of synthstone.

Ferus decided to ignore his instructions to land on the private landing platform of the prime minister of Samaria. Instead he headed for the main spaceport of Sath. He could always claim ignorance, and he wanted to get a feel for the city on his own, before he was briefed by some Imperial or government functionary.

"Boots logic," his Master, Siri Tachi, had called it. She meant get your feet on the ground, look around, and get a feel for the place yourself, instead of relying on the data you were given.

After landing, he activated the ramp and received a blast of heat from the dry air. He headed over to register with the dockmaster, a Samarian who waved him off. "You've already been cleared. The spaceport is closed to all vehicles but those with Imperial registration," he said. He turned back to the pile of durasheet records on his desk. "Can't believe I have to do this without a computer," he muttered.

"Why don't you just wait until the data is up and running again?" Ferus asked.

The Samarian looked up and blinked his mild blue eyes. "But then I'd be behind."

"True," Ferus said. He recognized a dedicated bureaucrat when he saw one.

"Take the turbolift down to the city levels. If you take an air taxi, you take your life in your hands. Space lanes are free-for-alls now. No controls at all."

Ferus nodded and walked to the turbolift. He took it down to the main level of Sath. It was a three-level city, with buildings of various sizes punching through the main street levels. Laid out on a grid, it had numerous ways for pedestrians to navigate with lift tubes, mobile ramps, and movers that could carry up to forty people at a time. All of the walkways were under cooling systems and shaded from the hot sun. Many buildings were connected by covered walkways at various levels. It was possible to walk the entire city without going outside. Fountains had been designed to refresh the air but were now shut off, no doubt because of the citywide system failure.

Ferus alternately walked and hopped on a repulsorlift mover. He saw disorder everywhere. Obviously the breakdown of the system had affected everything. The people were distressed, milling about, carrying on anguished conversation and desperately waiting in long lines. Considered highly advanced, the system on Sath didn't use physical credits, relying on computers to record every transaction, from a mug of tea to the purchase of a speeder. Now there were long lines at banks, clinics, and food distribution outlets. Frustrated Sathers crowded the streets, relying on barter to get what they needed.

Lighting systems were on half-power. Huge vidscreens that had once broadcast news and information were blank. The air lanes were snarled with traffic.

He could feel the panic in the air. This was a society on the brink of spiraling out of control.

Ferus finished his journey at the expanse of a blue-green bay. He hopped a repulsorlift ferry to take him out to the large, flowerlike span where the government residences were built. The heat was like a blast from a flamegun as he made his way down the empty boulevard.

He reached the gate to the palace and stood in front of the vidscreen, then realized it wasn't working. He looked around for a button to push or a comm device to activate but met only the smooth stone wall of the gate.

Then it slid open and he stared into the muzzle of a blaster rifle. The soldier was dressed in sand-colored fatigues. "State your business."

"Ferus Olin. I'm expected."

The soldier checked a durasheet. "This way."

Ferus followed him into the entryway to the palace. It was a large, sprawling white structure with seven domes inlaid with stone the color of the sea. Huge slabs of stone had been cut and placed in a striking pattern on the floor of the entryway. The glowlights were set in beautiful globes of blue glass.

Ferus followed the soldier into a reception area lined with long, low seating with tapestried cushions. He stood in the center of the tiled floor, a mosaic of a map of Sath. He looked down and reflected how fragile a mighty city could be.

He waited for fifteen minutes, until he realized he was deliberately being made to wait. Rather an odd way to treat an emissary from the Emperor. He had long ago learned — not from Siri, who could be so impatient, but from Obi-Wan — that part of diplomacy is never being irritated at being kept waiting, but using it to your advantage. So he used the time to study the map of Sath and memorize the main boulevards and districts.

At last the doors slid open and a tall man with graying hair entered. He was dressed modestly in a dark tunic and pants, and Ferus was surprised when he introduced himself as the prime minister of Samaria, Aaren Larker. He had expected someone in rich robes, someone who would match these opulent surroundings.

"Sorry to have kept you waiting," Larker said. "I was in conference with the Imperial advisor. He'll be along in a moment. I assume that you were briefed on Coruscant."

"I was briefed by the Emperor himself," Ferus disclosed.

"Imperial Advisor Divinian is here to oversee the

search for the saboteur," Larker said. "You are to work closely with him."

Ferus inclined his head. He had no intention of working closely with anyone.

"Divinian," he said. "Is that Bog Divinian, the former Senator from Nuralee?"

Larker nodded.

Ferus was surprised. He'd met Bog Divinian before the Clone Wars, when he was still a Padawan. Bog had been married to a friend of Obi-Wan's, Astri Oddo, but Ferus had lost track of both of them when he'd left the Jedi Order. Bog had fallen into disgrace after he'd conspired to take control of the Senate from Chancellor Palpatine. He'd been kicked out of office and scorned by his own people. How odd that the Emperor would allow him to gain such a high title, when Bog had once conspired to unseat him.

The doors opened again. Now Ferus realized fully why he'd been kept waiting. Bog wanted to make sure that Ferus knew that even though he'd been sent by the Emperor, it was Bog who was in charge.

"Ah," Bog said, by way of greeting. He held out a hand but didn't move. Ferus had to step forward to greet him. Bog was dressed in the gray tunic that most Imperial functionaries wore to match the soldier's outfits. Over it, he had thrown a royal blue cloak embroidered with gold thread. He had aged since Ferus had last seen him, ten years ago at the Galactic Games. His hair was dyed jet-black, and his florid face was now broad. His middle had thickened and his hair had thinned.

"Ferus Olin," he said. "Welcome to Samaria. I trust you found the Emperor in good health."

Ferus didn't think that "good health" would under any circumstances describe the Emperor, but he nodded anyway.

"The government of Samaria asked for our help," Bog said, folding his hands and putting on a grave expression. "Naturally the Empire was quick to reach out a hand. I am that hand," he said portentously.

Which I guess makes me a finger, Ferus thought. But he kept his mouth shut. It was important to keep Bog on his side, at least for now.

"The prime minister here seems to have lost control of his planet," Bog continued in a jovial tone. "Haven't you, old friend?"

Ferus saw the flush of annoyance on Larker's face. The contempt within Bog's tone made it clear again who was in charge here.

"How kind of you to elevate me to old friend when we've known each other such a short time," Larker said in a polite tone. Ferus strained to hear the sarcasm in it but could find none. Nevertheless he knew it was there.

"A friend in need, indeed," Bog continued. He wheeled and addressed Ferus. "You were supposed to land at the palace," he said.

"I wasn't aware I was under orders," Ferus replied.

Bog stared at him expressionlessly for a moment, then let out a booming laugh. "Just so! You're not in the Imperial army! So I suppose it makes sense to reject the advice of those who know better. The space lanes are dangerous in Sath."

"I walked," Ferus said.

This brought an incredulous look from Bog. "In the heat? I guess you're not aware that Samaria is a desert planet, ha-ha!"

Ferus was getting bored with Bog's attempts to put him in his place. He turned to Larker. "Have you had many problems with lawbreaking?"

Relieved to have his expertise consulted, Larker shook his head. "Not yet, but of course it is of concern. So far the Sathans are making the best they can out of a hard situation."

"Yes, I see that they're setting up a bartering system," Ferus said.

"We're working on establishing government-approved values," Larker said. "That way, everything will be clear, and the people will be able to figure out how to get food and fuel. That is our most important job at the moment. The saboteur has left no trace in the system. Every time we go in to try a fix, something else malfunctions. One day we'll have our transportation running, or our space lanes monitored, and then the next they'll be out again."

Ferus nodded. "I've seen this kind of bug before. If the saboteur is clever enough, it can be extraordinarily difficult to fix."

"I'm sure we'll be able to crack it," Bog said, obviously annoyed at being left out of the conversation. "Then we'll get everything under control."

Everything under his *control*, Ferus realized. This would be a test for Bog. Ferus would fix the problem, Bog would take the credit, rise in the Imperial hierarchy, and be the real power on the planet. It was a transparent plan, and the funny thing was that although Ferus was aware of it and Larker was undoubtedly aware of it, Bog still thought that his plan was shrouded in mystery. There was nothing worse, Ferus thought, than a dull man who was convinced of his cleverness.

But he couldn't underestimate Bog. He knew from experience that the combination of aggressiveness and ambition could make a being dangerous. Especially with the full might of the Empire behind him.

Now Ferus realized why he'd been sent. This wasn't about helping a planet — not that he'd believed that in the first place. Bog's presence here and the way he treated Larker made it clear: This was about taking over Samaria. If Ferus fixed their central computer system, he'd be giving the Imperials the method to control the planet completely.

CHAPTER FOUR

The spaceport at the city of Ussa on Bellassa was tightly controlled by the Empire. All arrivals and departures were monitored. Since Trever was wanted on his home planet, he needed to arrive with false ID docs.

Thank stars and planets, Trever thought, *for Dexter Jettster.* He had turned out to be a crucial ally for them. He was a member of the Erased on Coruscant, one of those who had completely wiped their identities in order to hide from Imperial security. Dex now lived in the Orange District on Coruscant, with access to the best identity thieves the planet had to offer . . . and that was saying something.

It had taken Dex less than an hour to pull together what they needed. He'd given them text docs and credits and a wardrobe — everything they needed to pose as a group traveling to Bellassa for its renowned spa treatments. Solace would be a wealthy woman, Trever her son, and Oryon their bodyguard.

To Trever's surprise, the no-nonsense Solace had agreed with the ruse, readily donning the fur-trimmed cloak and aurodium-colored boots of a wealthy woman. "Sometimes it's better not to sneak when you're breaking in," Solace said. "Make as much noise as you can, and nobody gives you a second thought."

Now Solace stood at the top of the ramp of the chromium-hulled starship that Dex had borrowed for them from a wealthy friend. She was resplendent in her rich ruby chaughaine robe. The black fur collar fanned out around her angular face. Instead of the scruffy warrior they were used to, she looked striking and regal. Trever wore a close-fitting cap made of some expensive material that itched.

He couldn't suppress a tremor of nerves as they waited to be checked in by Bellassan security. After all, he was wanted on this planet. He'd stolen a gravsled and pretended to be a laundry worker so he could break Ferus out of an Imperial prison. His image had been captured on a vidscreen. They could get touchy about things like that.

Dex had made sure he was well disguised. He was wearing a cap, and a large visor covered his eyes and most of his nose, a fashion among the young wealthy Coruscanti.

Solace created a stir around her, ordering security officers to hurry, and even hailing a corporal to carry her bag. Quickly she established herself as a presence to be placated. Security officers rushed to clear them, hurrying them to the front of the line and then quickly checking their ID docs against their list of those wanted by the Empire. Trever tried to appear bored, as if he were used to being coddled and swept through security.

The official looked over their docs with a skeptical eye. "You're here for the spa treatments? Haven't you heard about the unrest?"

"I came here for rest, not unrest," Solace said haughtily. "And I intend to find it. I'm not going to let some rabble-rousers come between me and my lasersalt rub treatments."

The official returned the docs. "Just don't go out alone."

"That's what I have my bodyguard for," she snapped.

They were cleared.

Trever's heart was tripping in his chest. It wasn't just about the fear of getting caught. It was about being on Bellassa again.

When he'd left his homeworld, he'd never wanted to come back. Stowing away on Ferus's ship was a way to escape a place that held only bad memories. His mother, father, and brother had all died here.

When they'd been a family, they'd always been together, going to concerts at the Ussa halls and outdoor venues, or playing laserball in the many parks. Almost any corner could suddenly blast him with a memory. He'd enjoyed being part of the black market, because it meant he could stay in a quadrant that was unfamiliar to him, rarely venturing into the neighborhoods he'd known.

But here was Bellassan air and Bellassan light, and they were as familiar to him as his own skin. *Home.* He fought against the concept, but here it was.

Another security officer rushed to hail them an air taxi. They entered, and Solace told the driver to take them to the Eclipse, the most exclusive hotel in Ussa. Trever had lived in Ussa all his life and had never been inside.

When they got to the hotel, the extraordinary service continued. Their luggage was whisked away, and check-in was accomplished in a matter of seconds. Soon they were stepping into a transparisteel turbolift that whisked them up to the two hundred and second floor.

Trever let out a disbelieving whoop as soon as the porters left them alone. He had a full view of Bellassa now. On this cloudless day, he could clearly see the seven lakes, the winding roads, and the pink and blue buildings in the soft, clear light.

"Can we stay here forever?" he asked. He was

joking, of course. But deep inside he felt a connection to this world. It hadn't been wrong to leave, but it felt wrong to stay away.

"Just a day," Solace said. "Maybe less, if they figure out the account number I gave them was a phony. Dex said we have about eight hours until it comes up blank."

"Let's get moving," Oryon said.

"What, no room service?" Trever asked with a grin.

They changed into less conspicuous clothes and took the turbolift back downstairs, leaving by a side entrance. Trever led them down the boulevards. His home city of Ussa had changed in the short time he'd been gone. The Imperial forces had cracked down hard after the entire city had rose in passive resistance against them. Stormtroopers were on every street. Security checks were set up on corners.

They passed a café where Trever and his family used to go on weekends. The waiter used to sneak him special sweets. Now Imperial officers crowded the best tables. . . .

He looked away.

"It's a sorry sight," Oryon said.

Trever shrugged. "This was never my favorite part of town, anyway."

Oryon gave him a quick look, his dark eyes piercing. Trever knew he hadn't fooled him one bit.

They continued on, Trever leading them through the winding streets. It was easy to get lost in Ussa if you weren't a native. The presence of stormtroopers grew less frequent, and though some prowler droids occasionally passed overhead, they must have been set on general surveillance, for they always moved on. Coded to intimidate rather than track.

Trever was leading Solace and Oryon to the hideout of The Eleven, the now-famous resistance group. Everyone on Bellassa knew about The Eleven, but not many knew how to find them. They were named after the core group who had started a resistance movement soon after the declaration of the end of the Republic. Roan and Ferus had been two of its founders.

The Imperials had quickly moved to establish a garrison on Bellassa, and the objections of the natives were met with fierce oppression and mass arrests. The initial number of eleven members in the group had grown until now it was rumored to be in the hundreds.

Trever's father had known Amie Antin, a doctor who treated the members of The Eleven. Trever had been one of the few allowed into their original hideout. He knew his father and brother would have joined The Eleven if they hadn't been killed by the Imperials during a peaceful protest.

The Eleven had chosen their hideout carefully, but it wasn't remote. The block was like all the others, neither too busy nor too deserted. Their house looked like the other family houses on the block.

"That's it?" Solace murmured as they approached. "We're in the middle of an ordinary neighborhood."

"That's the point," Trever said. "The Ussans have incredible loyalty to each other. The Eleven depend on that. Even if a neighbor suspected something they would die before they betrayed them."

"How do we get inside?" Oryon asked.

"We go in the back way."

Trever led them through a gate that was, surprisingly, unlocked. The path led them to a paved back area with a table and chairs. Beyond the sitting area was a wall with no door. Trever stood in front of it for a long minute.

"What are you doing?" Solace asked.

"Allowing them to see me. Amie Antin knows me. Wil, too. They'll let me in, even with two strangers."

"The trust of the Ussans," Oryon said.

"Exactly."

Part of the wall slid back, and they saw a ramp going down. The opening was big enough to hold a speeder. They followed Trever as he descended, and found themselves in a small holding area for vehicles. A door at the far end opened and a lovely woman of middle years with close-cropped white hair and dark eyes walked forward, smiling.

"Trever. You disappeared. Must I always worry about you?"

"Sorry, Dr. Antin. I decided to ship out and see the galaxy."

Amie shook her head. "Well, maybe that's not such a bad idea, considering how things are here. I'm glad to see you're well."

"My friends and I are here to help Roan and Dona."

"I guessed as much. We can use help. Come in."

Amie led them inside to a small interior room. Wil was sitting at a data screen. Trever saw that he'd been monitoring the backyard and the street, most likely to ensure that they weren't followed.

"Where are the others?" Trever asked, looking around.

"We've disbanded for the moment," Wil said. "They've spread out in the city. The Imperials haven't managed to completely subdue Ussa, but the crackdown gets worse every day. They're determined to control the planet. So we have our work cut out for us." He gazed at Solace and Oryon with polite curiosity. "What brings you to Ussa?" he asked.

Trever introduced Solace and Oryon. "We heard that Roan and Dona were arrested," he said. "Ferus sent us. He's well, but he can't come."

"Do you have any news of where they might have taken Roan and Dona?" Solace asked.

"Not much, and what we know isn't good," Wil reported. "We know they were taken aboard a ship. We've heard rumors through our spy network that the ship serves as a detention center and also a courtroom — so that political prisoners aren't tried on their homeworlds or indeed anywhere they can garner support. They are tried and sentenced in space, then taken directly to a prison world. The Empire can claim a fair trial but keep it all under wraps."

"The plan is for the ship to travel constantly through the galaxy, picking up political prisoners," Amie explained. "We have all our sources working on it, but we have no idea of its present location."

Trever felt his face fall. If Roan had been on Bellassa, they would have figured out a way to get to him. But the galaxy was a big place.

"Do you know where the ship left from?" Solace asked.

Wil nodded. "The main Imperial landing platform. They retrofitted a Corellian YT transport. It's called the *True Justice*."

"There's only one way to find it," Solace said.

"We have to infiltrate the landing platform and gain access to their tracking system."

Suddenly Wil's screen began to beep. Everyone looked at it in alarm.

A squad of stormtroopers marched down the middle of the street, peeling off in groups of five to investigate each house.

"House-to-house search," Wil explained. "New policy. They pick random quadrants of the city. Just bad luck." He turned to Amie. "We'll have to execute the abandonment plan."

Amie nodded.

Wil turned to the others. "We'll get you out, but we have a few procedures to follow."

"Can we help?" Solace asked.

"Thanks for the offer, but we'll be done in exactly fifty seconds. We've timed it out."

Trever watched as Wil quickly touched the data-screen, turning off all heat and light in the house. Amie hurried to throw large dustcovers over the furniture.

"We hope to fool them," she told Trever. "They'll think the owners are away."

Wil shut down the house in just a few seconds. He hesitated for a moment. "I have to clear the computer files," he said. "We have to leave everything out in the open, so it appears we have nothing to hide." With a sigh, he pressed the key that wiped the information off the house computer. "The only thing that remains will be normal transactions."

The stormtroopers were at the next house. They would be here in less than a minute.

They hurried back down the ramp to the hangar. Instead of taking one of the speeders, however, Wil accessed a hidden panel in the wall. It slid back, and he waited as the others passed through. They were in a small tunnel. The floor sloped downward and then made a sharp turn.

"We'll come out on the street behind the house," Wil murmured. "When they break into our house, they'll find nothing."

"Won't the fake back wall make them suspicious?" Solace asked.

"Only if they find it. We just have to hope they won't get suspicious enough to check out the back."

They reached another blank wall. Wil waved his hand over a hidden sensor. The wall slid back and they quickly slipped out into the cold gray afternoon. They were in an alley that ran behind a small landing platform that was shared by the neighborhood. Wil gestured to them, and they followed him into the deserted hangar.

"We keep a vehicle here, just in case," he said. "I think it's a good idea to get out of this quadrant."

They were heading toward the vehicle when

five stormtroopers suddenly entered. The leader's head turned. "ID docs," he ordered in his metallic voice.

"What should we do?" Amie murmured. "Bluff our way through?"

"If they find you with outsiders, it could compromise you," Oryon said.

"No talking allowed," rapped out the stormtrooper. The rest of the stormtroopers headed toward them.

"I can take care of this," Solace said.

"There's an entire squad," Amie said.

"Don't worry, she's not kidding," Trever said.

The stormtroopers raised their blasters.

Solace moved. She held out a hand and the Force slammed into the first two stormtroopers, knocking them backward. The remaining stormtroopers ran toward the group, but Solace was already moving, swinging her lightsaber in a clean arc that decapitated three with one blow. She kicked out with a foot, ducked, and turned in a complete circle and took out the leader and the remaining trooper.

Wil grinned. "You didn't tell us you were a Jedi."

Solace clipped her lightsaber back onto her utility belt. "You didn't ask."

"Let's get out of here," Amie said. "Another squad will show up before long."

They all squeezed into the speeder. "You should

lay low for a while," Wil said, shooting out of the hangar and steering away from the house-to-house search. "When they find the stormtroopers, they'll put a lockdown on the city."

"Good advice, but we don't have time to lay low," Solace said. "Take us to the Imperial landing platform."

CHAPTER FIVE

Ferus had been in the city systems computer center for hours now. The room hummed with the intricate panels and datascreens, all controlled by a giant droid known as Platform-7. It was a variant of a BRT droid computer, big as a room, especially built to run Sath. Here, everything having to do with the city functions was tracked — space lanes, glow-lamps, public fountains and parks, the power grid, the credit systems of all businesses. When the center had functioned smoothly, it had made living and working in Sath easy. Now that it was malfunctioning, it was almost impossible to trace where and how it had gone wrong.

Bog had stayed for only a short time, eager for Ferus to solve the problem. He'd become bored quickly and had left, with a hearty command to contact him as soon as he'd found the problem.

Ferus was no closer now to finding where the

worm had originated than he had been when he arrived. He stared at the datascreens with their streaming code, his eyes burning. He had expected cleverness, but this was diabolical.

Usually, computer thieves couldn't help but leave fingerprints, little eccentricities of code that you could follow if you knew what to look for. Some led to dead ends, but eventually he was able to follow the code back to the source. Not this time.

Ferus pushed away from the console and closed his eyes. This was a matter the Force couldn't help him with. He had a feeling he was going about this the wrong way. He couldn't use any of his old methods. He had to think in a new way.

Motive. Why would somebody foul up an entire city?

The first thing he thought was that they would attempt to steal a large amount of credits from the City Bank, where all transactions were recorded and all wealth was deposited. But that area checked out. No attempts had been made. He wondered if a citizen had been trying to get out of paying the heavy taxes most Sathans paid in order to live in such a smoothly functioning society, where all of their needs were met. But if that were the case, there was no way to track it. Along with birth and death records, the tax rolls were a mess.

Maybe the culprits were trying to cover

something up. Maybe it was revenge. Ferus spun around in his chair, trying to think. Without detailed knowledge of Sathan society, he couldn't begin to puzzle out emotional motives. He was reluctant to go that route until he had to. He'd rather attack the problem at its source.

Suddenly an idea made him bolt upright.

Ferus thought a moment, then typed in a span of dates, requesting city records for vehicle purchases.

Checking, the computer replied.

It didn't matter what the motive was. Whoever did this had to get off the planet. Ferus had a hunch. The Empire had shut down the spaceport in record time. What if the saboteur had intended to leave but was trapped on Sath?

If his luck was with him, the registration names would pop up. The random nature of the bug meant that some systems still worked, as long as no one checked them. He'd have a few seconds, that's all.

In minutes, a long list of names flashed up on the datascreen.

Ferus hit the buttons to print it out, but in reply his screen read, *Sorry, unable*.

It was the same answer he'd been getting all morning. By this time, he was imagining he heard regret in the computer's bland, agreeable tone.

He'd have to memorize the names, and fast.

Bog stuck his head in the door. "Any progress?"

"No," Ferus replied shortly. He moved through the names, trying to memorize them. It was similar to a Temple exercise when he was a Padawan. But he feared his mind had been sharper when he was a boy. Distracted, he moved through the list again.

Bog walked in and read over his shoulder. "Vehicle Purchase Registration Request Records? What does this have to do with anything?"

The names began to slither and slide offscreen, a sure sign that even though he'd been able to access them, another part of the system was now breaking down. "Nothing, and everything," Ferus told Bog. "I have to check each component of the city records to see if I can find the hidden bug." The names suddenly disappeared and the screen went blank. Ferus hit a few keystrokes.

Citywide waste delivery system now malfunctioning, the screen advised.

Bog's face went bright red. "You're supposed to be fixing the system, not making it worse!"

Ferus shrugged. Bog stamped out. Ferus turned away from the coding chaos on his screen. He had the names in his head. Now all he had to do was cross-check them. But he couldn't do it here.

He jumped out of his seat and headed for the door, waving his hand over the sensor as he moved so that he jumped through the hissing doors as they opened, surprising a stormtrooper just outside.

The stormtrooper snapped to attention. "I will contact Bog Divinian for you, sir. He just left. I can —"

"No need," Ferus said. "I'll be back."

He left the huge Sath Managing Complex and swung onto one of the main boulevards. Although Sath was a teeming city, he was now familiar with its layout. The main landing platform was less than a quarter kilometer away. He could sense a seeker droid behind him, no doubt tracking him, but he didn't care. There would be a time when he would ditch his surveillance, but it hadn't come yet.

He jumped onto the turbolift and hit the sensor for the landing platform. He strode out and found the same Sathan official in the Dockmaster Office. He was copying out names from the durasheets stacked on his desk.

"Leaving already? Don't blame you."

"I need some information. The day the saboteur struck," Ferus said. "When the Imperials closed the spaceport. How many were scheduled to depart?"

"Three hundred and twenty-seven," he said, without looking up.

"How many filed for a refund on the departure tax? Have you tabulated?"

"Almost all."

"May I see?"

The official hunted through the papers and handed a sheaf to Ferus. He quickly flipped through them. He immediately discovered the names of those who didn't file for a refund of the hefty departure tax.

The refund was a considerable amount of credits. Not many would turn down the chance to receive it.

He memorized the five names. One more stop and he'd be sure.

Thanking the official, he hurried back onto the turbolift. He took it down to the main level. There he hopped aboard a moving ramp that shot him forward. He could feel the presence of the seeker droid behind him.

Ferus took the ramp to the very center of the city. He exited and turned to the right, where a gleaming white structure loomed, long and low. This was the place where the Sathans mourned their dead. He walked inside.

The glowlamps were red and softly powered down, the air scented with herbs. The mausoleum wasn't staffed, but relied on huge datascreens for those who entered to find the name of their loved ones on the intricately carved, curving walls. By pressing the name, information about the loved one would appear and messages could be left.

The datascreens weren't working. But the names were arranged alphabetically, so Ferus was able to run down the curving walls, looking for a match to any of the five names he'd memorized. He found it in the Fs. There it was, Quintus Farel, just as he'd thought.

Quintus Farel had turned up in two places — on the list of those who had applied for a Vehicle Purchase Registration Request and on a list of those who never applied for a refund on the departure tax. If Quintus had bought a star cruiser and planned to leave, his plans had been foiled. But he hadn't bothered to get a refund.

All of this wasn't very interesting, except that Quintus Farel was dead.

He'd died twenty-five years ago at age two. A terrible speeder accident. His parents had died, too. Their names were beside him, here in the mausoleum.

Someone had stolen his name and ID information.

It was a common way to get an alias. Find a name that had already been recorded and it was easier to forge ID docs. A security number would have already been issued.

The saboteur had hit the personal records first — the birth and death records. They'd thought their tracks would be covered by the chaos that ensued.

But by cross-referencing the landing platform records — which an overly zealous bureaucrat had painstakingly kept on durasheets, unbeknownst to the saboteur — with the mausoleum records that were kept engraved on synthstone, Ferus had found his first clue.

"Gotcha," he murmured.

Before he left, he paused. The longer he let the seeker droid track him, the more information he'd be giving to Bog and the Empire. He wanted to find the saboteur himself, then decide what to do. He needed to make sure that he wasn't handing over the planet to Imperial control. He had to hope that Solace and Oryon would be able to find Roan and Dona and free them before he had to make a choice.

He stepped out into the street again. He felt the seeker lurking underneath the curved roof of the building.

Suddenly a skyhopper zoomed down in front of him. "Air taxi, sir?"

It was Clive. Ferus stepped inside the vehicle. "I've got a seeker droid to lose," he said.

"I'm way ahead of you, mate. You've been under droid surveillance since you left that crazy palace. Let's lose the creep."

Clive hit the engines hard. Ferus felt his stomach lurch as he moved up into space-lane traffic.

"Have to get past these canal bridges, then we

can go up," Clive said, swerving to avoid an air-speeder dodging an air taxi.

The space lane was clogged with traffic. Without signals, it was a free-for-all. Unfortunately, the citizens of Sath didn't believe in slowing down.

Ferus was plastered against the seat. "This is insane."

Clive cackled. "Isn't it great?"

The seeker was keeping up. Clive suddenly swerved to the left, nearly colliding with a large air-speeder. "Oops, I keep forgetting about my lack of starboard visibility." He tapped on the nav screen. "This keeps blitzing in and out."

"Great."

"Keep an eye out on starboard, will you?"

Ferus glanced over his shoulder. "There's an airbus —"

Clive pushed the skyhopper violently to the right, passing underneath the bus by centimeters. "I saw it!" he said defensively when Ferus gave him an incredulous look.

"Watch out for the —"

"I've got it," Clive said, diving down almost to the surface. "Woo, this is fun!"

"The seeker —"

"Oh, right." Clive yanked the controls and zoomed down an alley. He looked up. "Got some room over-head —"

"There's not enough room!" Ferus saw only a tiny bit of sky between a cluster of towers overhead.

Clive hit the engines, and the skyhopper zoomed up several kilometers in an instant. They passed through the space between the buildings, so close that the skyhopper scraped against the building. The vehicle shuddered, but Clive only went faster. They seemed to pop out of the space like a cork. Ferus could swear he saw the paint peeling off the hull of the skyhopper.

Below them, the seeker crashed into the side of one of the towers. It flamed out and dropped.

"Told you there was room!" Clive chortled.

He zoomed even higher, until they were in the upper atmosphere.

"Where to, sir?" he asked.

"The Hundred Seventh district," Ferus answered. "And step on it."

"Music to my ears," Clive said.

CHAPTER SIX

In an office in the Senate complex on Coruscant, a slender man clothed in black hit the control for his datapad. It rose from the center of his polished desk and he tilted the screen at the precise angle for viewing.

Senator Sano Sauro was impatient, but anyone peeking into his office would never know it. He sat composedly at his desk, his hands tightly folded in front of him. He hated to be kept waiting, and Bog Divinian was keeping him waiting. It was tiresome to have such a sloppy partner, but Bog had his uses.

He turned and looked at the artifact that hung suspended in a cube of transparisteel. He allowed himself to feel a surge of satisfaction at the battered object, a broken lightsaber hilt from a fallen Jedi. The Duro who sold it to him told him it had belonged to Mace Windu himself, but Sauro had no way to verify that. It just pleased him to imagine it.

He had hated the Jedi all his life. Their privilege, their arrogance. He'd brought one of them to trial — that odious boy, Obi-Wan Kenobi, who had later become such an important general. He was dead now, too.

And Sauro was alive. Older, but still in excellent shape, thanks to careful attention to his diet and visits to spas every six months. Not for him to accept the decrepitude of old human age.

He was now one of the most powerful Senators in the Emperor's inner circle, a confidant and an advisor. They had formed their alliance years ago, after his attempted takeover of the Chancellor's position. Palpatine had called him into his office after the debacle, when so many Senators had been slaughtered. Sauro had planned just how to wiggle out of responsibility. He'd blamed the assassination attempt on Granta Omega, of course, a conspirator who had gone much farther than he claimed to have known. He had expected censure from the Chancellor, perhaps an arrest, though there was no hard evidence. Instead, Sauro had been offered a deputy position. It was clear, Palpatine had said, that Sauro knew the uses of power. He would give him a platform to exercise that gift.

And he had.

Behind the scenes, he had bribed, punished, flattered, and manipulated. Now he was the unseen power behind Palpatine. The Emperor had been hideously scarred after the assassination attempt by the Jedi Mace Windu, but Sauro did not underestimate him. His personal power had not diminished.

The problem was his new enforcer. Darth Vader had appeared out of nowhere. Sauro felt him like an electrojabber in his side. Vader was standing between him and the Emperor, and he couldn't have that.

Vader was consolidating his power, planet by planet, system by system. He was bringing governments in line. Already his name was spoken with fear.

Sauro didn't know where Vader had come from, but he knew he wasn't a politician. He didn't know how to maneuver his way through powerful blocs and strategic alliances. In the end, that would bring him down. He was just a thug.

Palpatine needed someone with elegance and subtlety. Someone like him.

Sauro believed in careful plotting. He didn't act in haste. He needed to outmaneuver Vader, but it would take time. It might take years. He would wait. If Vader was proving to be the Emperor's enforcer, Sauro would be the Emperor's strategist. Eventually he would demonstrate to Palpatine that he should be his second in command, not Vader.

The trick was to find out what he needed to do to impress Palpatine. He had to go above and beyond what he'd done in the past. He had to anticipate. Not answer the needs of yesterday, but the needs of tomorrow.

He was good at that.

His comlink signaled at last. The miniaturized hologram of Bog beamed onto his desk.

Bog bowed. "Everything is going according to plan, good friend."

"And what does that mean?" Sauro asked. Bog was always vague. He seemed to think that if he wasn't pinned down, he could be seen as marvelously efficient.

"The Jedi is under surveillance. The sensor tag adhered to his boot as he stepped forward to greet me, just as I'd planned. Unfortunately a seeker droid tracking him — because I believe in backup — met an unfortunate accident. Smashed into a building. The traffic in the space lanes is unruly because of this situation —"

"You idiot, it smashed into a building because the Jedi wanted it to," Sauro said. "It wasn't an accident. If you've got a sensor in his boot, what do you need a seeker for? He'll spot it no matter what it does. Just track him with the sensor. Where is he?"

"In the Hundred Seventh District. It's in the northwest area of the city —"

"I don't care where it is — I want to know if he's found anything!"

"Hard to know," Bog said.

"It's your job to know," Sauro said irritably. "Find out."

He cut the communication abruptly. He'd have to monitor Bog more closely. Sauro himself didn't get where he was today by underestimating a Jedi, even a failed Jedi like Ferus Olin.

He swung his datapad closer. He tapped on the keys. He was taking no chances. He doubted that Ferus Olin was following the Emperor's orders without his own plan.

Sauro placed a secret code in his files. A neat booby trap. If someone tried unauthorized access, he'd know it immediately.

No one must be allowed to interfere with his plans.

CHAPTER SEVEN

Wil and Amie dropped Solace, Trever, and Oryon off on a bluff overlooking the Imperial hangar and adjacent landing platform. Due to the large number of vehicles and troops needed for the garrison, it had been built on the outskirts of Ussa, on an empty plain that stretched toward the foothills. Solace, Oryon, and Trever lay flat, watching the traffic below.

"If we can get to the holding pen for the airspeeder transports, we can go in that hangar door," Solace said. "It's not being used that much."

To Trever, it looked as though it was being used every few minutes. Leave it to a Jedi to say something was easy when it was so clearly impossible.

Solace gave him one of her rare smiles. "I can see you doubt me."

"I never argue with you or Ferus," Trever said. "What's the point?"

"Good philosophy." Solace slipped her liquid cable out of her utility belt. "Ready?"

Oryon nodded. "I'll take Trever."

Great. The next thing Trever knew, he was hanging on to the strong broad back of Oryon and falling through thin air, the wind whistling past his ears. They landed on the ground with a bump. They were concealed here by boulders, and they quickly snaked through them until they were close to the hangar door.

Two stormtroopers were conferring near the entry. After a moment, they both turned to walk inside.

Now, Solace signaled.

She ran across the few meters of open ground. Trever followed, expecting at any moment to be blasted into oblivion. But they reached the safety of the wall. Solace peered around the corner into the interior of the hangar.

She signaled, and slipped inside. Trever followed. The hangar was connected to docking bays that ran the length of the structure. Arcs of durasteel rods held the plastoid retractable roof in place. They stood behind an equipment loader and scanned the space.

The place was mainly staffed by Class Five labor droids. Binary load lifters were busy with cargo.

Freight droids moved smaller durasteel bins filled with weapons. Battle droids handled the security.

"This is why they won," Oryon said. "Look at this place. They're so efficient they can build this in no time at all."

"They cut corners, though," Solace said. "Antiquated docking system, no fuel lines to individual hangar bays."

Oryon gazed overhead. "No automated fire protection."

"Why bother? They can afford to lose droids and stormtroopers."

"We need to get to a dataport," Oryon said.

"It's best if they don't know we broke in," Solace said. "I could take out the droids, but . . ."

"What we need is a diversion," Trever said.

"Sure," Oryon agreed. "But what?"

Trever glanced around the hangar. A group of labor droids was using a welding tool to fix a battered speeder. The sparks flew as they busily wheeled about. Next to them was a fuel storage bin and a parked gravsled. A power droid was nearby, its generator humming as it recharged several smaller freight droids.

"Give me thirty seconds," Trever said.

Ducking around speeders and ships for cover, he raced toward the droids. When he got within tossing distance of the fuel storage bins, he reached into his utility belt. Carefully modifying an alpha charge, he lobbed it toward the first bin. The tiny explosion was covered by the noise of the hangar.

The charge blew a small hole in the fuel container. The fuel began to dribble out. It formed a small stream that snaked toward the sparking tool. Trever backed up slowly, then dashed toward Solace and Oryon.

He felt the explosion at his back. It lifted him through the air and slammed him down on the permacrete. He felt his breath leave his body.

"Galactic," he breathed. He rolled over and took cover.

Droids converged by the fire. With no automatic fire protection equipment or hoses, they had to scuttle back and forth between the fire stations and the blaze. The labor droids turned to monitor the situation, but the confusion overwhelmed them.

Oryon was already moving, leaping toward the dataport. Solace moved to guard him in case he was spotted. Trever decided to stay where he was. He watched Oryon's fingers fly over the datakeys.

Something alerted him, a flicker at the corner of his vision. It was a security droid, trying to get a fix on his position. Trever reached for a charge in his belt, but Solace had already seen the droid. She leaped up to slash it in two with her lightsaber.

And just like that, they were spotted.

Security droids wheeled and advanced, firing at them. Oryon raced from the dataport, Solace covering his retreat with her lightsaber. She moved like wind and water, with no trace of effort. Her lightsaber was a revolving circle of light. Trever waited, knowing that Oryon and Solace would come for him.

They did, running quickly, Oryon's blaster firing, Solace's lightsaber arcing and moving. Trever tossed a few half alpha-charges and then ran.

Solace motioned to them and they charged into a small shuttle. Oryon jumped behind the controls. Trever leaped for the laser cannon. He blasted away at the droids as Oryon fired up the engines and they zoomed out of the hangar and shot up into the atmosphere. In moments, the landing platform was a spot on the surface of the planet. A thin trail of gray smoke marked where the fire was.

"So much for not attracting attention," Oryon said.

"Can't be helped," Solace answered. "Did you get any information?"

"Not enough," Oryon said. "The ship's location is coded, and I didn't have enough time to break it. I did learn something interesting, though — the ship is the pet project of a Senator named Sano Sauro. There's a direct comlinkage between his office and the vehicle."

"Never heard of him," Solace said. "I stay away from Senate politics."

"He's in the Emperor's inner circle," Oryon said. "A nasty piece of work. Maybe Keets and Curran can help us from their end."

"I'll send them the information," Solace said, taking out her comlink.

"Sorry I couldn't get more," Oryon said.

Trever looked around the cabin. "No sweat. At least we got a nice ship."

"There's nothing more we can do at the moment," Solace said. "We'll have to play hide-and-seek with the Empire for a while. We'll see what Curran and Keets can come up with."

CHAPTER EIGHT

The atmosphere at Dex's hideout was tense. Dexter Jettster had finally left Curran and Keets alone in the study, unable to put up with their bickering. They were going through information sheets on any link between Samaria and either the Senate or the Empire, and it was rough going. There was plenty of information to study, but no links that stood out. The search was wearing on both Keets's and Curran's nerves. They both needed to be doing something, and this felt like a waste of time.

After Solace finished her brief request, Curran shut off the comlink. He fixed Keets with his sharp, penetrating gaze. His nose twitched.

"What did I do now?" Keets threw a wadded-up paper from a muja muffin on top of the pile of durasheets on his table. He brushed the crumbs off his tunic.

"We almost missed that communication. The comlink should be available at all times."

"I handed it to you!"

"After a search. You lost it under that pile."

"True. But I found it again. You never give me enough credit." Keets grinned at Curran. "You want the rest of my muffin?"

"I don't . . . want . . . the rest of your muffin." Curran articulated each word. "I want you to be responsible."

"I keep telling you, don't say that word while I'm in the room. What did they say?" Keets asked.

Curran sighed. He sat down carefully in a chair after brushing off some crumbs. "They couldn't locate the ship, but they did discover an interesting connection. Sano Sauro is in comlink touch with the ship."

Keets whistled. "That *is* interesting. It's our Bog Divinian link. He's a protégé of Sauro's. Do you think they're cooking up something on Samaria?"

"No doubt. If we can find out what, we might be able to help Ferus and get some crucial information to Solace and Oryon as well."

Keets looked at his messy table. "I knew there was a reason I was going through these senatorial records. Every time Divinian, that pompous son of a bantha, makes a move, Sauro is somewhere in the background."

"Sauro plucked him out of obscurity and brought him back to the government," Curran said. He smoothed the fur on his cheeks with his hands, a gesture he made when he was thinking hard. "He's risen fast. But Divinian is nothing more than a hack. Why would Sauro need a hack?"

Keets gestured at the pile of durasheets, sending half of them shooting off the table. "Bantha Bog isn't his only hack. He's got plenty more." Keets thought a moment as he gazed at the pile on the floor. "At first I thought Sauro just didn't have good judgment. His protégés are the emptiest heads you've ever seen. Find a being, male or female, who's been raised with wealth and hasn't done a thing with it, shove them into positions of power . . ."

"And then control their every move," Curran said. "You're really the one with the power, not them."

"He's personally handpicked Imperial advisors to at least ten planets in the Core that I know about," Keets said.

"But how does this help us with Samaria?"

"It doesn't . . . yet," Keets said. "But it's brilliant, if you go in for that evil mastermind sort of thing. Sauro has managed to ingratiate himself into Palpatine's inner circle. Now he's consolidating his power outside of it. I'd bet he's going to butt heads — or should I say helmet — with Vader eventually."

Dexter Jettster stuck his big head in the room. Two of his hands gestured at them. "Have you two stopped going at each other like a pair of nek battle dogs or have you found something?"

"Just a plot to take over the galaxy," Keets said.

Curran blew out a short breath, ruffling his facial fur. "Sano Sauro is handpicking Imperial advisors and sending them to strategic planets in the Core Worlds. He's also set up a ship called the *True Justice*, a kind of traveling courtroom for political prisoners. That's where Roan and Dona are being held."

"Good — finding them is the first step." Dex stroked his chin with one of his four hands. "Setting up a system to try political prisoners is a smart move. That would give him access to any information on resistance movements."

"And he's a special advisor to the new academy where they're starting to train pilots and officers," Keets said. "He's got a finger in a lot of nasty Imperial pies."

"In another few years, he'll have planetary rulers and officers loyal to him, as well as all the Senators he has in his pocket," Curran said.

"The question is, does Palpatine know what he's up to?" Keets asked.

"Might know, might not care," Dex said shrewdly. "He'll let Vader handle Sauro if he has to get rid of him. In the meantime, he's helping the Empire. But how does this help our friends?"

"We know he's in constant communication with the *True Justice*," Keets said. "So at least we can send the coordinates to Solace."

"Break into his files at the Senate?" Dex asked. "The two of you are well known there. You got away with it once, but sneaking into a senatorial office will be harder. Zackery is still in charge of security."

"Zackery! My old friend," Keets said. "We had many a tussle when I was a reporter. I got thrown out of the Senate building by him more times than I can count."

"He's nothing to laugh at," Dex advised, with a frown. "More power has just made him meaner. This is a dangerous game, my friends."

"The only kind to play," Keets replied.

CHAPTER NINE

Most of the population of Sath lived in tall high-rises, some luxurious, some not. The building Ferus was looking for fell somewhere in the middle range. It was built overlooking a canal, and a large landing platform crowned a hangar nearby.

"Decent place, but what are we doing here?" Clive asked as they zoomed up in the turbolift.

"All vehicles applying for departure must register an address with the landing platform," Ferus answered.

"So you think the person using Quintus Farel's identity is here?"

"No. I think whoever sold him the cruiser is here. I think he was able to use the address of the former owner because it hadn't been changed in the system yet."

"I never realized what a mind for details you had, Ferus."

"It's an old skill."

"Must have made you popular."

"It made me a bore."

Ferus pushed the door alert button to an apartment on the fiftieth floor. He stood in front of the security screen. In a moment a voice squawked out of the speaker next to it.

"What is it?"

"I'm here to ask you a few questions about a star cruiser you sold several weeks ago," Ferus said.

"If there are any problems with it, they aren't mine," the voice snarled. "When I sold it, it was in top condition."

"No, no problems. Can you open the door? It would be easier to talk face-to-face."

A hesitation, then the door slid open. A young woman stood before them, her shimmersilk dressing gown knotted tightly around her waist. She looked Ferus and Clive up and down. "Okay, here's my face. What is it?"

"I have some questions about the person you sold the cruiser to. Quintus Farel."

"So ask. Do I look like I have all day for this?"

"Did you meet Quintus Farel?"

"You're not from Sath, are you? Who meets anybody in this city? I placed an electronic advert, this Quintus answered it, we exchanged details, I got credits in my accounts, Quintus got the ship. I bought it for some romantic space travel, but my boyfriend took off, the dinko. Anyway, who wants to travel in this galaxy now? Stormtroopers, everywhere I look."

"Did you ever speak directly to Quintus?"

"Once. I parked the cruiser in the wrong space by mistake, so he couldn't find it. I forgot to move it. Sue me. So I got a comlink call from Quintus, I think he was afraid I was going to cheat him. It wasn't my fault, my neighbor parked in my space, the monkey lizard."

Suddenly Ferus had an idea. "Are you sure Quintus was male?"

She shrugged. "Deep voice, and it sounded electronically altered. Mr. Secrecy. All I cared about was the transfer of credits into my account."

Ferus wasn't getting much information out of the woman. Clive gave Ferus a look that said, *Let me take over.* He put one hand on the door frame and smiled down at her. "I can see you pay attention to things. Did Quintus mention where he was going?"

The woman rolled her eyes. "Why would he do that? And why would I care? Get your hand off my door."

Clive straightened, no longer trying to work his charm. "How long is the range of your ship?"

"No hyperdrive, if that's what you're asking. But it was fast. I like to go fast. Are we done?"

Ferus sighed. "Thank you for your time."

Discouraged, he and Clive turned and started back toward the turbolift.

"Was that the rudest woman in the galaxy, or am I crazy?" Clive muttered under his breath.

"You're not crazy."

Then they heard her call them. "Fellas?"

They turned back.

"Just thought of one thing," the woman said. "The comlink communication came from the Fountain Towers."

"How do you know?"

"Well, the blocking mechanism was on, so an address didn't pop up. But the Fountain Towers complex is new. Nice place, wish I could live there, but I'm stuck in this hole. It surrounds the Seven Minerals Fountain, in the Three Hundredth district."

"But if the address was blocked —"

"I'm not finished. The Seven Minerals Fountain has a chord clock — every half hour, it strikes the first three chords of the Samarian anthem. I heard that. So I'm guessing Quintus lives in the Fountain Towers. Because he was pretty annoyed at me and said he had to go all the way home again without the ship."

"I could kiss you," Clive told the woman.

"Not tempting," she said, shutting the door.

Ferus pressed the turbolift sensor. "What now?" Clive asked. "If this Fountain Towers place is anything like every other building in Sath, it's got hundreds of apartments."

"And a hangar next door, if we're lucky. A space cruiser will be parked in a numbered space," Ferus said. "We have him."

The turbolift whooshed downward, stopping every once in a while to pick up more passengers. As it descended to the lobby, and the passengers disembarked, Ferus put his hand on Clive's arm to slow him down before he exited behind them.

"What is it?" Clive asked when the passengers had exited.

"I have a funny feeling about this," Ferus said.

"That Force of yours?"

Ferus nodded. "We're being followed. I'm sure of it."

"We lost the seeker droid." Clive took a few steps into the lobby. The floor-to-ceiling glass windows afforded a view of canal and street and sky. "Nobody out there that I can see. . . ."

Ferus walked forward cautiously. Then he stopped. He raised one foot, then the other. He ran his boot along the stone floor and heard a slight clicking noise. "A sensor tag," he said. "It's on the sole of my boot."

Clive squatted down. "Clever." He straightened. "But we're cleverer."

"That's not a word."

"Sure it is. Come on."

They walked out of the building. They hesitated, watching the passing air traffic.

"That one," Clive said, pointing to a shining chromium speeder that was barreling down the space lane, cutting off other vehicles as it swerved.

"Just what I was thinking."

Ferus Force-leaped up to the canopy that overhung the ten-story lobby. He hesitated, balancing on the edge. As the speeder approached, he plucked the sensor off his boot and sent it spinning. It connected to the rear of the speeder. In a moment, the speeder had disappeared around a bend.

Ferus jumped back to the ground, doing a somersault on the way down.

"Show-off," Clive said.

"Come on," Ferus said. "I'd guess we have about an hour before Bog figures it out. Well, knowing Bog, we might have more than that."

Quickly they headed to the skyhopper and took off. They stayed in the space lanes for the short trip, and Ferus had another hair-raising ride. He was happy to see the Fountain Towers rising against the cityscape.

The towers were built on the edge of the city, far from the wide aquamarine bay. There were four slender towers, and each had an adjoining hangar that was almost as tall. The hangars contained open-air landing platforms every twenty stories. Three of the towers were completed, and one was half built, its hangar just a shell. The upper levels of the building were full of scaffolding and exposed beams.

They landed near the fountains, which were now dry. Clive zoomed into the first hangar and parked the skyhopper. They began the tedious process of tracking the registry numbers of the vehicles.

At last, they found the vehicle on level fifty-eight. Ferus peered inside the cockpit.

"Clive, look at this," he called.

Clive pressed his face against the cockpit bubble. "Wow, a control panel. What a surprise."

"No, in the passenger seat."

Clive looked again. "It's a laser lasso."

"A toy." Ferus frowned. "I didn't think there would be a child involved." Ferus had a bad taste in his mouth.

Something didn't feel right. It hadn't felt right since he'd stepped foot on this planet. He was being manipulated. He was sure of it. But why? Why had Palpatine chosen him for this mission? Ferus had a pretty good idea of his own skills, but he knew he wasn't the only being in the galaxy who could help with this problem.

. The closer he got to finding the saboteur, the more uneasy he became.

"Maybe this isn't the ship," Clive said.

"No, this is it," Ferus said. "I feel it. And look — there's some mud rubbed on the registry numbers to try to obscure them. It's an old trick, but it works."

Ferus gazed over at the apartment tower, thinking. He knew that Solace would contact him as soon as she'd rescued Roan and Dona. Until then, he would have to keep going, keep following one step after another until he found the saboteur. Whether he handed the saboteur over to the Imperials or not was another question — one he hoped he wouldn't have to answer.

CHAPTER TEN

Even in the middle of the night, the Senate never shut down completely. As Keets and Curran made their way down the hushed hallways, they passed cleaning crews who didn't give them a glance, bleary-eyed senatorial aides hunched over their cups of strong tea, and Senators, resplendent in their opera cloaks, stopping by after an evening out to pick up records for the next day.

But Sano Sauro's office was dark.

Keets used a nifty device Dex had loaned him. It fit into the palm of his hand, making it unnotice-able as he pressed it against the sensor panel. With a few beeps, the device broke the code, and the door slid open.

"Sure wish I had this when my landlord kept locking me out of my apartment," Keets said as he slipped it into his pocket.

"Why did he do that?"

Keets stepped through the doorway. "Oh, a little thing called *failure to pay rent.* Landlords are touchy creatures."

They slipped like shadows into Sauro's inner office.

"He's a tidy fellow," Keets said, looking around. "I don't trust anyone this neat."

"I'm not interested in his character at the moment," Curran said, crossing to the desk. "Just his files."

Keets followed at a more leisurely pace, as he checked out Sauro's spare collection of items, the curved horns the color of blood, rising from the edges of his desk. "Old habit, my friend. Investigative journalist. Sometimes I'd learn more from what was in someone's office than what was in his files. Like this." Keets paused before what looked like a sculpture, the only decorative object in the room. It was a metal object with a crack down the middle, suspended by a small repulsorlift motor in a clear transparisteel cube.

"What is it?" Curran asked as he searched for the dataport release button.

"A lightsaber hilt." Keets circled it slowly. "He hates the Jedi. He keeps the symbol of their defeat in his office, right in front of his eyes, so he can see it every day."

Curran found the release. A datascreen rose

from the middle of the desk. He quickly ran through the files. "Coded."

"Naturally. Allow me." Keets slid into the chair and tapped at the keyboard. "I'm in."

"That was fast."

"It's all in the wrist." Keets expertly keyed in a phrase. "I'm going to search any files that were recently opened. . . . Whoa, what's this?"

"What's what?"

"A memo Sauro sent to Palpatine. Blah blah, your excellency, your Imperialness, the usual . . . but here. He promises results on Samaria. *'Personally responsible for results,'* he says . . . blah, more drivel, and — wait. Here. He says, *'and there will be news of a deep interest of yours that has long coincided with mine.'* What could that mean?"

"I don't know," Curran said. "But let's concentrate on the *True Justice*."

Keets returned to searching through files. "Here we go." He converted a file to holographic mode and sent it into the air.

Together they leaned closer to scan it. It was a complete record of the *True Justice,* complete with schematics.

"We need a ship's log for coordinates," Curran said anxiously.

"Not a problem — we'll find it," Keets muttered. "Wait. Something's wrong. I've tripped something."

"What?"

"A security code. Here — see that shimmer on the indicator light? Some models of this dataport display that if it's been booby-trapped. It's supposed to be a silent alarm, but if you know where to look . . ." Keets glanced up at Curran. "We'll get caught."

"Yes."

They exchanged a quick look that confirmed what they had both decided. This information was vital. If they were caught, so be it.

Keets continued to flip through the file, moving even more rapidly now. "Here it is."

Curran moved to the door. "I hear them."

"I'll transmit the entire file to Solace." Keets keyed in the coordinates. "First I have to copy it. If I send it from Sauro's computer, they'll be able to track her."

"They're close."

"Almost done."

Keets watched the streaming file. Every second counted.

"They're in the outer office!"

Keets saw the blinking *FILE COPIED.*

The door slipped open and Senate security poured in, Imperial guards led by one short, burly human man.

"Well, hey there, Zackery. Long time, no —"

"Keets." The man pointed a blaster. "Breaking into a Senator's office again, are you?"

"Keeps them honest." Behind his back, Keets's fingers were working frantically, keying in Solace's comlink access. He pressed the comlink and sent the file.

"I'm going to enjoy handing you over to the Empire."

"Anything that makes you happy," Keets said. He glanced at Curran, giving him a look that told him the transfer had been successful. It didn't matter what happened to them now. They'd won this round.

CHAPTER ELEVEN

"They did it," Oryon said. He stared at the data-port on the Imperial ship. "They've given us coordinates, scheduled stops, even a schematic. I'm going to stop underestimating Keets right now. I'd better send back a thank you."

"Don't," Solace said. "Look at the last code. It's our emergency signal. They were captured."

Oryon, Solace, and Trever stared at each other. "What should we do?" Trever asked.

"Our duty," Solace said. "We get to the ship and release Roan and Dona."

Oryon took a deep breath. He walked over to the pilot's ship and entered the coordinates. "They're close to Bellassa," he said. "It shouldn't take us long. But we have a couple of problems."

Solace nodded. "How to board, for one."

"And we're on a stolen Imperial ship," Trever said. "They're probably looking for us."

"Don't forget I was a spy," Oryon said. "I can program the shipboard computer to randomly change our registry number every few minutes. They'll never get a fix on us. Eventually they'll figure it out, but we just need a little time."

"Good," Solace said. "Now we have to plan our boarding."

She bent over the files again, quickly scanning the information.

"It could work," she murmured. She looked over her shoulder at Oryon and Trever. "We have to take the chance."

"What chance?" Trever asked. When Solace looked at him like that, he began to feel nervous. The look said, *Are you up for this?*

"There's an Imperial judicial team — an attorney, a judge, and a law clerk — scheduled to board at the Penumbra Spaceport," Solace said. "They're to conduct the trial of Roan and Dona. If we went directly to the ship, we could fly right into the cargo hold. We could pose as the team and get aboard."

"Wouldn't the real team contact the ship when the ship never showed up for them?" Oryon asked.

"We'd have a couple of hours. We could free Roan and Dona and control the ship," Solace said. "This idea is so new that Roan and Dona are the only prisoners. It's mostly staffed by droids."

"Yeah, a new model of security droids," Trever pointed out. "The ones with dual laser cannons."

"Not so easy," Oryon said.

"I didn't say it was easy," Solace said. "But it's our only chance."

Trever stirred nervously as Solace guided the ship to a landing hangar inside the Imperial ship. He had no idea what a law clerk actually did, or how a law clerk would speak or act. He had no doubt that a law clerk would be smarter than he was. Maybe it would be a good idea to keep his mouth shut.

Oryon spoke to him in a soft voice. "The trick is to believe you are what you say you are."

"That's some trick."

Solace activated the ramp and turned to them. "Just follow my lead," she said.

They walked down the ramp. An Imperial officer waited for them.

Solace nodded at him shortly. "I am Judge Bellican. This is Attorney Tomay Alcorn and clerk Sam Weller."

"First Officer Dicken. Follow me."

The officer led them to the cockpit. The captain sat in the control post. He stood as they came in and Officer Dicken introduced them. "We understood that you'd meet us at the spaceport," Captain Tran said.

"Change in plan," Solace said. "There are compelling reasons to speed up the trial."

"I'd like to see the prisoners," Oryon said.

"They're in lockdown. The trial will begin in five minutes."

"That does not give me enough time to prepare a case —" Oryon said. The plan had been for them to release Roan and Dona as soon as they could.

He was interrupted by the captain, who gave him a sharp glance. "But these are standing orders for the ship. All prisoners will be tried immediately upon the arrival of the legal team. The point of this new system is speed and efficiency. I understand you've already prepared the case."

"Of course, but there are always last-minute details. . . ."

"I was fully briefed by Senator Sauro. I expect you were as well."

"Yes," Solace said quickly.

"Then a droid will see you to the courtroom. First Officer Dicken and I will act as witnesses for the official record."

There was nothing to do but nod. Solace and the others left the cockpit and followed a protocol droid into the hallway.

"What are we going to do?" Trever hissed.

"Exactly what we're supposed to," Solace said. "We're going to try Roan and Dona."

CHAPTER TWELVE

The courtroom was a small conference room with no chairs for spectators. Why would there be? The trials were designed to be conducted in secret, with the prisoners escorted as quickly as possible to prison. Stormtroopers and security droids were lined up against one wall, no doubt to keep any possible agitation from turning into violence.

Solace sat in the judge's chair, on a slightly raised platform at one end of the room. She quickly familiarized herself with the controls. "I have the capability to activate the droids," she whispered to the others. "That should come in handy."

Two tables faced the judge, and Trever and Oryon took their places at one of them.

Captain Tran and First Officer Dicken hurried in, followed by a law droid, who took its place at the other table.

The captain and the first officer stood at the back. Obviously they didn't think this would take long.

"Let's hurry this along," the captain said. "We've got to finish this and make it to the Nunce system to pick up a load of prisoners. My job is to fill up the ship, and the sooner I do it, the sooner I get a better commission."

Roan and Dona were led into the courtroom by guard droids. Trever looked at them carefully for signs of mistreatment. Dona looked thin and tired, but Roan walked in, his head high. He saw Trever and gave a small start, not visible to the officers. Then his face was impassive again.

"This trial will come to order," Solace said, hitting an electronic gavel that emitted a soft *bong*.

Roan and Dona sat at the table with the law droid.

"Roan Lands and Dona Telamark, you have been accused of conspiracy against the government of Bellassa and plotting to assassinate the Imperial advisor to the government of Bellassa. How do you plead?"

"Guilty," the droid said.

"Wait a minute," Roan said. "This hunk of junk doesn't speak for us. We requested a lawyer."

"I am a court-appointed attorney, sir," the law droid said, swiveling its head.

"This is outrageous. Under rules of the Galactic Senate, we have the right to choose our own counsel."

"I must correct you, sir," the droid said. "The Emperor has suspended that right in Senate Act three-two-one, point seven, when it comes to traitors of the Galactic Empire."

"But I haven't yet been proven a traitor of the Empire," Roan pointed out.

"Yes, but we have the right to try you as one."

"If you are, indeed, my attorney, then I have the right to fire you," Roan said. "I'll handle our case."

The droid's head swiveled faster, its sensors flashing. "There is no precedent for this. I must do a more extensive search of my memory banks."

"Don't bother," Solace said. "The accused has a point. I recognize his right to fire you."

The law droid's sensors blinked frantically. "Objection!"

"On what grounds?"

"On the grounds that it violates the procedural microchip!"

"Overruled. Let us proceed."

"What's going on here?" Captain Tran asked.

"I'm sorry, Captain, you are a witness to this proceeding, not a participant," Solace said. "I accept Roan Lands as attorney. How do you plead?"

"Not guilty."

"Let's get this show into the space lane," the captain muttered. "I have things to do."

Solace nodded to Roan. "Proceed with the prosecution."

Roan stood. "Before we begin, I make the motion to dismiss the case, your honor. This case was built on illegal surveillance. Under the rules of the Bellassan Senate, an order from a security court judge must be obtained. This was never done."

The droid's sensors blinked. "Objection! The Emperor has suspended the need to obtain an order to run surveillance on any citizen of any world in the galaxy for any reason."

"True," said Solace. "But the Galactic Senate has not ratified the decision."

"But it hasn't been asked to consider it," the droid protested. "The Emperor doesn't need permission."

"Nevertheless, I feel this is a gray area," Solace countered.

"This is contrary to the information in my procedural memory banks," the droid said. "Highly irregular . . . overheating circuits. I must be repaired immediately!" It quickly bolted from the room.

Captain Tran stamped his foot. "Gray area!" he exclaimed, exasperated. "There are no gray areas in the Galactic Empire! The Emperor has done away with gray areas! That was the problem with the Republic!"

"May I remind you to keep quiet, Captain?" Solace asked. "Political speeches are out of order in the courtroom."

Oryon stood. "We recognize the prisoner's legal point. Upon careful review of the case, your honor, I respectfully submit that the charges against the accused be dropped."

"This is outrageous!" the captain blustered.

"I am the judge," Solace said. She hit the gavel gong. "Case dismissed! Furthermore, I charge you, Captain Tran, and your first officer Dicken with obstruction of justice — and mutiny."

"Mutiny!"

"Mutiny, sir, for interfering with an Imperial court case." Solace pressed the security droid button. She pointed to the stormtroopers. "Take them to lockdown."

The captain reached for his blaster, but Oryon was there in less than a moment. He pressed his own blaster against the captain's temple. "I'd rethink what you were about to do."

"But you have no right!"

"When we walked on board, we gained that right. We represent justice in the Empire," Solace answered. "Surrender your weapons."

Captain Tran and First Officer Dicken handed over their blasters to Oryon.

The security droids and stormtroopers began to march them from the courtroom. "You'll be hearing about this," the captain said to Solace and the group. "You're all going to wind up in an Imperial prison!"

"Looks like that's where you're headed!" Trever called.

As soon as they were out of the room, Dona slumped at the table in relief, but Roan laughed. "Thanks for the save."

"We're not safe yet," Solace said, leaping to her feet and taking off her judicial robe. "We're going to have to take the ship."

"Let's go," Roan said. "Anybody have a blaster?"

Oryon tossed him one of the three blasters.

Dona stood. Color had flooded her face, bringing her strength and vitality back. "Who are you people?"

"Wait, let me guess. Friends of Ferus?" Roan asked.

"Good friends," Oryon said. "I am Oryon, and this is Solace. You already know Trever. Ferus is safe, but we'll tell you about him later."

"I'm willing to take over an Imperial cruiser," Roan said. "No problem. But aren't we about to meet a bunch of enraged droids? And we're only five?"

"And one of us is a bad shot," Dona put in.

"We got the schematics of the ship," Solace said.

"It runs with a light crew. Most of the droids are kept in the hold. They're only there in case of attack. If we can take control of the cockpit, we can lock down the hold."

"How many will be in the cockpit?"

"About three officers and twenty droids," Solace said. "It won't be a problem."

"Did she just say it's not a problem?" Roan turned to Oryon.

"Trust me," Solace said.

They strode out into the hallway. Solace took the lead.

They hadn't gone very far before a protocol droid met up with them. "Crew awaiting captain's orders," it said.

"The captain has been arrested," Solace said. "I am in charge."

"That's a violation of authority," the droid said. "I'll have to summon —"

In a flash, Solace moved forward, lightsaber in hand, and sliced his head off.

"Oh, dear," the disembodied head said.

With an expert slice, Solace disabled its control panel even as she continued to race down the hall.

"Ah, now I get it," Roan said. "Ferus found his Jedi."

They raced down the hallway, following Solace to the cockpit. Trever was impressed at how quickly Roan integrated himself in the group. He moved to Solace's right, letting Oryon cover her left. Dona stayed behind with Trever. The five of them weren't exactly an elite attack group, but Trever had no doubt they would win.

Solace activated the doors of the cockpit and charged in, lightsaber in hand. The new security droids began to fire their laser cannons, raising their forearms. Fire pinged through the cockpit in streaks of energy. Trever dropped and rolled.

In less than a minute, Solace had sliced through three droids and somersaulted in the air to knock down another before burying her lightsaber in its control panel. Then she reversed to take down four droids standing guard. Oryon and Roan took care of the rest.

The cockpit was now filled with smoking droids and fused metal, and Solace had her lightsaber pointed at the chest of the officer in charge. "You don't want to push me, do you?" she asked. She wasn't even breathing hard.

"What do you want?" he asked.

"We'll give you safe passage to a spaceport. All crew must depart. We'll leave you with your lives if you leave us with the ship."

The officer shared a glance with his crew. "I'm not dying for this ship. I agree."

Oryon sprang to the controls. Roan held his blaster on the three Imperial officers as he settled into a chair and crossed his legs. "I'm going to enjoy this ride," he said.

CHAPTER THIRTEEN

Keets and Curran sat in the Senate retaining room, where those who violated security were kept. They were relieved they hadn't immediately been shipped off to an Imperial detention center.

Zackery sat at a table, watching a broadcast of a gladiator droid contest on his datascreen, ignoring the prisoners. Keets considered whether to overpower him, but he knew there was additional security behind the closed door. They were waiting for something, and he had a feeling he knew what it was.

The doors hissed open, and Sano Sauro appeared. Despite the fact that it was the middle of the night, he was dressed and groomed impeccably.

Zackery sprang to his feet. "Here they are, sir. We caught them red-handed in your office."

"Leave us."

"But they could be dangerous. . . ."

"I hardly think so." Sauro plucked a piece of lint off his black sleeve. "Go."

Zackery left hurriedly, tucking his datapad under his arm.

Sauro seated himself at the table and folded his hands. "Who are you working for?" he asked.

"No one," Curran said.

"Don't waste my time. Either you tell me or I hand you over to Imperial interrogators. From what I understand, you," Sauro said, turning to Keets, "were a third-rate journalist, and you," he continued, turning to Curran, "were a low-level Senate aide until the Empire was established, after which it was determined that you both had violated the laws of the Empire, and warrants were issued for your arrests."

"Third-rate?" Keets reared back. "You can torture me all you want, but there's no need to call me *third-rate*."

Sauro's gaze was dark and neutral. "I have enemies," he said. "I accept that as an inevitable part of power. It is necessary for me to know who they are. Now, you will either tell me or you will be forced to talk by an Imperial interrogator. *Who hired you?*"

"Bog Divinian," Curran said. He didn't think it was possible to surprise Sano Sauro, but he saw the flicker in his gaze.

"You're lying," the Senator challenged.

Curran didn't answer. It was enough to have planted the suspicion in Sauro's mind. Better to keep Bog and Sauro off balance and not trusting each other.

"I don't have time for lies," Sauro said, rising smoothly, "so I —"

The door hissed open behind him. Sauro didn't turn, but they saw his anger at being interrupted.

"I didn't summon you."

Zackery took a hesitant step into the room. "Urgent communication for you, sir. The *True Justice* has been hijacked."

"You fool, tell me outside!" Sauro's face was white.

Keets kept his face impassive, but he could have cheered at the look of fury on Sauro's face. The guy was panicking, that was for sure.

And he had no doubt that Solace and Oryon and Trever had done the impossible: They had freed Roan and Dona.

"Do not tell anyone this news," Sauro hissed at Zackery. "It must not reach the Emperor." He turned back and looked at Keets and Curran with hatred. "I'll deal with them later," he said. Then he hurried out the door.

CHAPTER FOURTEEN

Darth Vader was used to being called to Palpatine's office at any hour, so he was not surprised at the summons that called him there in the predawn hours. He didn't need much sleep now. If not for the demands of what was left of his body, he wouldn't sleep at all. Sleep brought dreams.

He found his Master standing at the window overlooking the lights of Coruscant. It was where he plotted his strategy. They had done so much, but power gained must still be consolidated. How thrilling it would be at last to hold the galaxy firm in a fist, to know that because of his efforts it would run smoothly, without the petty systemwide wars that had plagued it in the past, without the inefficiency of many voices clamoring for different things.

"Things are not going well on Samaria," the Emperor said without preliminaries. "I haven't troubled you about it because it seemed a minor problem. Yet Samaria is necessary for us, a strategic link to the rest of the Core."

"I am not surprised, my Master," Vader said. "I did not understand why Divinian was put in charge."

"There are reasons to keep him occupied," Palpatine said.

"Sano Sauro."

"That is one reason. Sauro is useful. He is trying hard to please me. He sent me a secret memo about the Academy."

Vader waited. Sauro was not a problem, not yet. He knew well that Sauro would plot against him. Sauro was more annoying than threatening.

"He has an idea," the Emperor said. "It's about Force-sensitive children."

Vader grew alert.

"We have eliminated the traitorous Jedi, but not the Force-sensitive. Sauro claims he is the only one in the galaxy who has the ability to discover a Force connection in children." Palpatine gave a mocking smile. "Can you imagine the arrogance? He had a protégé, long ago — a fallen Jedi named Xanatos."

"He was once the apprentice of Qui-Gon Jinn. He turned to the dark side."

"I knew of him, but he was not my apprentice.

Sauro said that Xanatos told him many secrets of the Jedi. He knows about midi-chlorians."

Vader was keeping his anger in check. "He inflates his importance."

"No doubt. But he thinks this will please me. He doesn't know that he is dealing with a Sith. It's quite amusing to listen to him."

"What does he want?"

"To bring Force-sensitive children to the Academy," Palpatine responded. "He believes that the Force can be used to train pilots. Reflexes, instincts. He thinks in ten years we could develop an invincible fleet."

"He doesn't understand the Force," Vader said. "You can't train children to develop the Force as *pilots*." He spit out the last word in disdain.

"This, from a former Podracer?"

Vader didn't move. He knew his Master brought up his childhood from time to time to test him, to prod the place that was most painful.

"Of course you are right," Palpatine said. "But I am going to let him have his little idea — for now."

Vader knew better than to disagree with his Master, but he had to make his objection. This news troubled him. He did not want other Force-connected beings to be gathered together. Order 66 had eliminated the Jedi. He thought they were gone forever.

"It is a waste of time," his electronically-enhanced voice said.

His Master turned to him then, and once again Vader saw the extent of his power. Palpatine knew him down to the bone.

"If it makes you uncomfortable, you can find your own way to stop it," Palpatine said. "You and Sauro are headed for a showdown. It is up to you to choose when it will take place. I will not interfere."

"Yes, Master."

"I have just received word that the *True Justice* has been stolen. Sauro thinks I am unaware of this."

"This is another example of his poor planning," Vader said. "A ship can be more vulnerable than trying prisoners in a court."

Palpatine waved a hand. "It was an interesting idea to try. But this is why I have called you here. Sauro is overextended. He has to find that ship and cover his tracks. He cannot afford to take care of Bog Divinian."

Vader guessed what was coming. "So I must?"

"You must control the situation. Samaria must be ours."

"It will be done, Master."

Vader turned and walked out, his cape sweeping behind him.

Palpatine heard the doors hiss shut.

He had worried his apprentice. Darth Vader did not want Sauro to gather any Force-sensitives. Especially children. It would serve as reminders of things he thought he needed to forget.

He didn't need to forget them.

He needed to glory in what he had done.

He needed to scorn what he had lost.

Sauro would not be successful in his quest. He was not as clever as he thought. Only a Sith or a Jedi could find a Force-sensitive. Perhaps Sauro could stumble across one or two and point to his success. It did not matter.

What mattered was Ferus Olin.

The Emperor laughed. All Masters tested their apprentices from time to time.

This would test Darth Vader most of all.

CHAPTER FIFTEEN

Quintus — or whoever was posing as the deceased Quintus — was behind the door. The question was how to get in.

"Why don't we just knock?" Clive asked in a whisper.

"They'll have an exit plan," Ferus said, disagreeing. "Can't you break in?"

"I'm insulted. I'm not a thief! Do you really think I can break a security door?"

"Just do it."

"All right." Clive reached into the pocket of his tunic. He withdrew a small fusioncutter, a coin, and a sharpened piece of plastoid. He bent over the security keypad with the items. Within seconds, the door clicked open.

They entered silently. They were in a short hallway. A door to a fresher was off to their right.

Ferus waited, listening, searching for evidence of the Living Force.

"No one is here," he said.

"How do you know?"

"I know." He walked inside the apartment. It was sparsely furnished. He carefully looked around, then crossed to the small kitchen and opened cabinets.

"Hungry?"

"No one is living here. But someone is trying to make it look that way."

"So it's a dead end."

Ferus crossed back to the living area. He looked out the window to the skeletal unfinished tower next door. "I know where to look," he said.

The turbolift shafts had not been completed. There was only an exterior lift for the workers to access the roof. Ferus and Clive took the stairs. The workforce was on the roof today. They could hear the noise of turbohammers dimly echoing through the building.

Ferus followed the trail as though he was tracking someone through the woods. He saw the imprint of work boots in the dust from the construction, but he was looking for something unique — the footprints of a child.

He found them on a landing on the twenty-second floor. He lost them on the thirtieth and found them again on the thirty-sixth. At last he stopped on the sixty-second floor.

There were only four apartments per floor. One had no door and was still being worked on. They were now on the highest partially completed floor. Ferus listened at the door of the remaining three apartments. "This one," he said. "Open it."

Again Clive worked his magic and the door slid open silently. They took a few cautious steps into the empty hall.

They heard something, a murmur of a female voice.

They moved closer.

". . . And that doesn't mean you don't keep up with your lessons."

A boy's voice. "But I don't have any teachers."

"I'm your teacher now. Do it or you'll turn into a horned hairy urchin toad."

The boy giggled.

Ferus and Clive exchanged a look. It sounded like a typical exchange between a mother and a child. Could this be the home of the daring saboteur? Ferus risked a quick look around the corner.

The room was bright with light and furnished with only a table and bright cushions on the floor. On the floor sat a young boy of about eight years, with dark hair. He was bent over a datapad. Cross-legged next to him was a woman with close-cropped dark hair. She was dressed in a flight suit.

She looked up, and there was no fear in her gaze when she saw Ferus. Her hand drifted to her side.

"I wouldn't do that," he said softly.

Her hand stopped. He saw the glint of a blaster, concealed in the pocket of her flight suit.

Something about her face was familiar. What was it? He knew her. He had a sudden memory of a woman with tumbling dark curls.

"You're Astri Divinian," he said. "Bog's wife."

She rose smoothly. "I'm Astri Oddo. Bog is no longer my husband. This is my son, Lune. Who are you — and how did you get in?"

"We met once, years ago. Very briefly. At the Galactic Games on Euceron. I was with the Jedi team that supervised the games. Ferus Olin."

He saw her response in her quickened breathing. "A Jedi? That's impossible. They were all . . . wiped out."

"I left the Jedi Order years ago."

He watched as she moved to block Lune. She did it casually, as though she were edging closer to study him. Astri had been a great friend of the Jedi. Why would she consider him a threat? He felt something. . . .

Something . . . He reached out with the Force, searching . . .

"Have you come to arrest me?" she asked. Behind her back, she put a hand on Lune's shoulder.

"I don't work for the Samarian government, or for the Empire," Ferus said. "But I was asked to find you."

"By whom?"

"That's not important." Ferus crouched down in front of Lune. He held out his hand. The laser lasso was in his palm. "Did you lose this?"

"You found it!" The boy took it from him. "I didn't know where it was." He unfurled it, and it snaked around the room, fast and agile. He lassoed a small cushion and sent it flying, somersaulting through the air. He laughed.

"Lune! Don't do that." Astri's voice was tight.

Ferus turned to her. "Is there somewhere we can talk?"

"The kitchen." Astri turned to Lune, and in a soft but firm voice said, "Stay here and finish your lesson."

The three adults moved into the tiny kitchen. Ferus could feel Astri's fear. He just wasn't sure what, exactly, she was afraid of.

Despite her fear, she turned to them defiantly. "Did Bog hirc you?"

"No," Ferus said. "Does he know you sabotaged the computer system of this planet?"

She was at first surprised, but then shook her

head. "He doesn't know I'm involved. I doubt he'd think I was capable of it."

"Lune is Force-sensitive."

She bit her lip. "Yes."

"How long have you known?"

"Since he was four. I had my suspicions, let me say. He was different . . . the way he anticipated things. Obi-Wan once told me the story of Anakin Skywalker. I remembered."

"Does the boy know?"

Astri shook her head. "He knows he's different. That's all. Bog didn't know for a long time. I left him shortly before the Clone Wars, after the attack on Chancellor Palpatine. I knew Bog was involved. I knew he'd tried to discredit the Jedi in the Senate. And I knew," Astri said, her eyes dry, her mouth tight, "that he would take my son to punish me."

"What happened?"

"My father, Didi, died during the war, and we came here. Bog somehow got into power again and he used that power to find me. I let him see Lune against my better instincts. One day they were play-ing, and Lune . . . he suspended a laserball in midair. Bog realized what it meant. Now he wants him . . . for something, something for the Emperor, I don't know what. I only know he wants to take him away."

"Wait a minute," Clive interjected. "You sabo-taged the records of an entire planet so that your ex-husband won't get his hands on his own son?"

Astri's dark eyes flashed. Ferus had forgotten how lovely she was. He remembered that she'd been very close to Obi-Wan. He wished he could tell her that Obi-Wan was still alive. But that was a secret he could not share with anyone.

"Bog fathered that child but did not raise him," she said angrily. "He had no interest in him except as a bargaining chip to keep me in line. We haven't been able to leave the planet. Now he wants to take him from me to curry favor from the Emperor. He is to be raised on Coruscant, he told me."

"But you've thrown the whole planet into chaos, endangered lives," Ferus said. "Medical records have been lost, financial records . . ."

"All to protect one boy," Clive said.

"Yes," she said. "I would do that to protect one boy."

Ferus leaned against the kitchen counter. What was he going to do? How could he sacrifice Lune? Astri didn't know the Emperor was a Sith. If she knew that, she would fight even harder.

If he turned them in, Lune would be raised with evil. He could even become a Sith . . . or killed like the Jedi had been killed.

"I'm begging you," Astri said. "Can you please let us go?"

Ferus suddenly felt off balance. He crossed to the window and looked out but saw nothing. Yet he knew. The Force was warning him.

Since they'd been in the building, background noise had hummed — the noise of airspeeders landing in the adjacent parking garages, of turbohammers on the roof.

Clive had noticed it, too. "It's awfully quiet."

"Something is wrong," Ferus said. "The dark side has arrived."

CHAPTER SIXTEEN

Ferus left Clive with Astri and took the stairs. He Force-leaped down, going from one landing to another. He could feel the heavy, enveloping dark side of the Force like a shroud over the building. He had one overwhelming thought: A Sith was near.

He stood inside the stairwell and cracked the door to the unfinished lobby. The work vehicles were gone, as were the gravsleds and the camis. Suddenly he caught a glimpse of a prowler droid. He followed the droid's flight until it landed . . .

. . . and found Darth Vader leading a squadron across the courtyard.

They must have just arrived. Darth Vader, his cloak billowing out behind him, was instructing teams of stormtroopers and giving orders to droids. Prowlers were sent flying in the air.

Ferus took the stairs again, soaring into Force-leaps that brought him back up to Astri's door faster than a turbolift.

He hurried inside. Astri and Clive were still in the same place in the kitchen.

"We've got trouble," he said. "It's Darth Vader. He's directing a door-to-door search. Stormtroopers are guarding the exits, and droids are conducting the search and entering the hangars. There looks to be at least fifteen or twenty prowlers, too."

"There are hundreds of apartments," Astri said.

"This is Darth Vader," Ferus said. "It won't take him long. The good news is that he's starting with the inhabited buildings."

"So, how do we get out of here?" Clive asked.

Astri looked at both of them. "You won't turn me in?"

"We won't," Ferus promised. He tried not to think about Roan. He had to have hope that he had already been rescued.

"If we can get to the Tower One hangar, I have a star cruiser," Astri said.

"The droids will be all over the hangars," Clive said. "And if we go out the front, the stormtroopers will get us."

"There is always a way," Astri said.

Ferus looked at her, surprised. "That's what Obi-Wan used to say."

"He was my friend, too," she said with a sad smile.

CHAPTER SEVENTEEN

"We have a problem," Oryon said. "I've checked the comm system, and there's no way we can send a message to Ferus. It will get picked up by Sauro."

Solace leaned over the holographic map. "We're close to Samaria. We could just go there."

"It's closed to everything but Imperial traffic."

"We *are* Imperial traffic."

"I have no doubt," Oryon said, "that they know we've hijacked the ship. I'll change the ID profile and hope for the best."

"Change it to an Imperial diplomatic ship," Solace advised. "Come on, Trever. Let's find some uniforms."

Trever left the cockpit with Solace. They searched several storage rooms and came up with Imperial officer uniforms for everyone. Quickly, the group pulled them on.

It wasn't long before they approached the landing

platform at Sath. Oryon transmitted their identification. They waited. They all knew that if their ruse didn't work, they could be blasted right out of the sky.

"If they don't answer soon, we go in anyway," Solace muttered.

Just then the confirmation code flashed. "We're in," Oryon said.

Trever looked down as Sath drew closer. The city looked impossibly big. "How are we going to find Ferus?" he asked.

"We'll find him," Solace promised. "We can activate the homing signal on his comlink now that we're on the same planet."

The dockmaster gave a quick look at their ID docs and waved them through. "All checked in, watch out in the space lanes, controls not functioning today," he said in a breath and hurried off.

They went down into the cargo hold and piled into the cruiser. They zoomed out into the chaotic space lanes of Sath. Solace took the pilot seat, confidently zigzagging through the snarled air traffic. As they approached the coordinates, she slowed down, then made a wide turn around the Fountain Towers.

"Something's going on down there," she said.

"Those are security vehicles," Oryon observed.

"Stormtroopers," Trever said.

The ship dipped down. "I'm going in," Solace

said, parking it close by but out of sight range of the building lobby. They piled out.

"Just act like you belong," Solace said.

Dressed as Imperial officers, no one stopped them as they headed purposefully into the building. Stormtroopers were stopping any residents and requesting ID docs as they arrived or departed, but Solace's group was waved through.

"Ferus is here somewhere," Solace murmured.

Trever suddenly saw something that made him feel as though ice had been dumped down his neck. "Vader," he said. "Over there."

They ducked down a hallway. Solace crept back to survey the situation.

"Vader is leading the search," she said. "We've got to find Ferus first."

CHAPTER EIGHTEEN

"We've got to go up," Ferus said.

"There is no up," Astri told him. "There are just beams up there. No access to the hangar."

"That's where we have to go," Ferus said. "We'll just have to figure out a way to get across to the hangar. Can Lune make it?"

"He's just a boy!" Astri protested.

"I can make it, Mom." The boy stood in the doorway, looking suddenly more mature than his years.

Astri's face softened. "I know you can."

They started as they heard a rapid knocking on the door. Clive reached for his blaster, as did Astri.

But Ferus smiled. He knew that knock.

He hurried down the hall and opened the door. Solace, Oryon, Trever. And Dona and Roan.

He and Roan grabbed each other's upper arms in their special greeting. "You're free!" Ferus said.

"Thanks to your friends."

"We couldn't contact you from the ship, so we thought we'd just drop by," Solace said, striding in. "I assume you know Vader is downstairs."

"I decided to wait before I said hello to him," Ferus said.

He quickly filled them in on who Astri was and what they had to do.

"Can we all fit in your cruiser?" Solace asked her.

"It will be a squeeze, but I think we can manage it," she answered.

"Since we're wearing Imperial uniforms, we might be able to leave with extra passengers," Solace said. "We've got an Imperial ship waiting at the spaceport, but there's no telling when they'll double-check our landing docs."

Astri looked relieved. "That solves the problem of how to get out of the planetary atmosphere. They'll blast Samarian ships, no questions asked. Luckily everyone has obeyed the order."

Solace halted and gave Astri a keen look.

"I don't believe you told us everything," she said. "Sure, you'd do anything to protect your son. But you wouldn't put other beings in danger, would you?"

"The people of Samaria are inconvenienced, but not in danger," Astri admitted. "I acted with the permission of Aaren Larker."

"The prime minister of Samaria?" Clive asked.

Astri nodded. "Larker was the one who concocted the plan to sabotage the data system. We saved the med records and secretly transported them to the hospitals and doctors. Larker hired me to do it — ever since leaving Bog, I've made a living as a programmer."

"You're one of the best slicers I've come across," Ferus said, using the galactic nickname for a talented computer code expert.

"I took the job because I wanted to help, but I also wanted to disappear. One of my conditions was that I could wipe my identity and Lune's records from the Samarian system. I thought I'd take off right after, but I was delayed, and then the Empire closed the spaceport so fast. . . ."

"They can be very fast when they want to," Clive said.

"So why did Larker do it?" Ferus asked.

"He knows that the Empire is planning to take over the planet. He decided to break down the system in order to give the Sathans time to form a resistance cell. When the system comes back up, some records will be gone, such as who fought on the side of the Republic in the Clone Wars, or who criticized Emperor Palpatine when he was still a chancellor. They'll have to start from scratch to find their enemies."

"Enough talking," Solace said. "Let's move."

Astri put her hand on Lune's shoulder. "We're ready."

Ferus squatted in front of the boy. "Lune, we're going to have to climb on the roof and walk across a beam. We'll be very high."

"I have good balance," the boy said.

"I'm sure you do. When we're up there, I want you to try something. Trust your feelings. Try not to think, only feel. Let the air help you."

"What he means is —" Astri started.

"I know what he means, Mom," Lune said. His gray-blue eyes were clear as he nodded at Ferus.

Ferus nodded back. A connection passed between them, one he knew was fueled by the Force. Someday, he hoped, Lune would know what that meant.

They walked out of the apartment. They could hear the whistling of the wind around the girders on the roof.

"Stay back!" Solace suddenly said.

She and Ferus turned at the same moment as two prowler droids crashed through the hallway window. The two Jedi leaped up as one, and slashed through them. Smoking, the droids crashed to the ground.

"They had time to transmit our position. We have to move quickly," Ferus said.

They raced up the stairs. The wind hit them full in the face as they stepped out onto the partially completed roof. Girders and beams crisscrossed the area closest to the hangar in the adjoining tower. Ferus stayed close to Lune and kept a careful eye on Trever.

He and Solace concentrated the Force. This was a difficult task for any Jedi, especially one who had never achieved Master status. To lift a heavy object in the air using only the Force took great concentration.

No, Ferus told himself, remembering the lessons of Yoda. *Not concentration. Belief.*

The beam rose in the air, rotated, and traveled across the empty air to the hangar tower next door. It entered one of the openings and shuddered as it hit. It held.

They now had a bridge to cross over. Hundreds of kilometers in the air, with no railing . . . but a bridge.

"Solace, you lead Astri and Lune over," Ferus said.

Astri and Lune balanced on the beam. The wind blew, pushing Lune's hair in his eyes. He didn't flinch. He appeared perfectly balanced.

"I'm letting the air help me," he called to Ferus.

"You can do it," Ferus said.

Solace stayed between them. They walked single file across the beam. Lune never faltered. He never looked down. He walked across the beam as though he was strolling across a park on a sunny day.

"Now I've seen true courage," Clive said.

Ferus turned to agree that the boy was amazing. He saw that Clive was watching Astri.

Solace, Astri, and Lune reached the other side. Astri hugged her son to her side.

"Your turn, Trever," Ferus said.

Clive crooked an arm for Dona. "I'll escort you to the beam, madam."

Dona nodded. "Don't worry about me — I live on a mountain. I can do it."

Trever, Dona, and Clive started across the beam.

Roan waited with Ferus. They watched as the trio inched across the beam.

Suddenly Ferus was alert to an intruder. A prowler was streaking toward the beam. In the hangar tower, Solace had seen it, too. Dona ducked, almost losing her balance, but Clive grabbed her arm. Another prowler zoomed upward.

"Don't move!" Ferus shouted to Roan. Then he Force-leaped across the space, soaring toward the aggressors as Solace did the same. In midair, the two Jedi slashed through the droids, sailed past each other and both landed on the beam as lightly as drifting snow.

"Ferus!"

Roan was leaping from beam to beam, avoiding beam fire from two spider droids that had appeared on the partially finished roof. Ferus jumped back to the roof, deflecting the fire. He landed behind the two spider droids and slashed at them with his lightsaber, turning them into molten metal.

"I'm beginning to like this Jedi business," Roan said.

Across the way, Trever, Dona, and Clive were now safe in the tower. Roan and Ferus hurried to the beam and walked quickly across. "Okay, now comes the hard part," Ferus said.

"My cruiser is three levels down," Astri whispered. "The ramps are at each end."

They moved toward the ramps that linked the levels. They couldn't risk taking the turbolift. They were almost down the ramp when they heard a squad of stormtroopers heading up. It was too late to retreat; the troopers had spotted them. The commander gave the order to fire.

Ferus and Solace raced forward as the troopers began firing. Their lightsabers whirled as they charged. Roan and Oryon stayed behind, firing their blasters. Clive and Astri placed themselves in front of Dona, Trever, and Lune, their blasters in hand.

Ferus was not used to fighting with Solace. Her

style surprised him. She was a loner, and, at this point, a reluctant Jedi. But her fighting style was as generous as it was aggressive. Her leaps were liquid, and she seemed to be everywhere at once, protecting Ferus and guiding them all downward even as she vanquished the troopers. Ferus couldn't read her intentions as quickly as he should, but it didn't matter. She read his. She countered his moves, reinforced his strikes, and covered his back.

When the clones were littered around them, he deactivated his lightsaber and nodded at her in admiration. "Thanks."

They continued on, down to the next level. More prowler droids flew toward them, and Ferus cut them down in three clean strikes.

"They're going to send more firepower now," Solace said. "They know where we are."

They raced down the last ramp toward the cruiser. Solace leaped into the pilot seat. Dona hurried inside along with Clive. Oryon sat next to Solace. Roan jumped in behind Solace, squeezing himself into the cockpit behind the laser cannon controls. Astri and Lune were next.

Suddenly an explosion rocked the hangar. A pair of droidekas had entered and were blasting at a load-bearing column. The column soon crashed to the floor.

The roof overhead began to cave, cracks spreading rapidly. The duracrete underneath their feet began to shift. Ferus grabbed Lune with one hand and Trever with the other. Oryon reached out and yanked Astri inside the craft.

"Lune!" Astri screamed.

With a thunderous roar, half of the level above collapsed. Ferus dove for cover with the two boys as the droidekas continued their deadly blasts.

Solace gunned the engines and soared away from the flying debris. She hovered outside in the air while Roan manned the laser cannons. He made one accurate shot, blasting one droideka and sending the flaming mass of metal into the other one.

Ferus rolled to his feet, coughing out the dust. "Discord missile!" he shouted, spotting one in the air. He knew from his Clone Wars service that it was filled with a flock of buzz droids, those lethal droids that could adhere to a starfighter going at top speed and drill into it, disabling it in seconds.

Solace dove away, but the discord missile kept tracking.

Lune suddenly sent his laser lasso flying. It was a clean red line in the air, flying outward toward the missile. Ferus held his breath. He could feel the Force in the air as Lune unknowingly used it to guide the lasso. Lune may not have been aware of what the Force was, but his mother was in danger and he would make it work for him.

The lasso snaked around the missile, hard enough to yank it slightly off course. It crashed into the side of the hangar. Solace zoomed away, under fire from the ground now.

More stormtroopers were spilling up the ramp, blaster rifles firing. Ferus released Trever and kept the two boys behind him as his lightsaber arced in the air, deflecting fire. While he moved backward, he considered what to do. Solace was circling around, trying to avoid fire and get back inside the hangar. The battalion was between her and Ferus. More were coming every moment. One of them fired a missile and it hit only meters away. Ferus felt the heat of the blast on his face.

Thinking frantically, Ferus jumped onto a small airspeeder. He shepherded Trever and Lune inside, then started the engine. "Drive!" he ordered Trever. He leaped onto the back of the speeder, lightsaber in hand, and deflected fire. Trever took off.

"Where to?" Trever shouted.

"The roof next door!" Ferus dropped back into the speeder as Trever pushed the engines. They shot out into the air and straight over to the roof. Here they were finally out of range of the blasterfire and missiles.

"Let me take over," Ferus said, reaching for the controls. He zoomed over the beams, searching. Then he dove the craft down into an unfinished turbolift shaft. Safe for the moment, he let the craft hover.

"What now?" Trever asked.

Ferus thought carefully back on the design of the tower. He knew the wall would be thin near the roof, since the reinforcing durasteel hadn't been added.

"Solace will find us," Ferus said. He directed the craft up the shaft and maneuvered it closer to the wall. "I need you to do something for me."

Trever saw the order in Ferus's eyes. He shook his head. "No. I'm not leaving you. Not again."

"You have to. You have to take Lune."

"I can take care of myself," Lune said.

Trever sighed. He knew he had to go. "Every time I leave you, you end up captured."

"Not this time. The Emperor wants me free. I don't know why, but he needs me. All I have to do is walk out. I can buy time until you can get away. Trever, it's the only way."

Trever nodded. "All right. But just so you know, you can't get rid of me for good."

"I know." Ferus activated his lightsaber. He buried it in the wall. It glowed, and the wall began to disintegrate, peeling back on itself. Lune watched, wide-eyed.

"I've never seen a Jedi in action before," he said. "I wish I could do that."

"Maybe someday you will," Ferus said. He jumped onto the partially demolished wall. Hanging on with one hand, he scanned the air. He was high over Sath, on the opposite side from the lobby. Stormtroopers were specks below him, lined up and ready to receive orders. Several seeker droids zoomed below but hadn't tracked him yet. He saw no sign of Darth Vader but still felt his presence.

A glint on a wing, and Solace was diving, heading for him.

"You're going to have to be quick," he told Trever.

Trever balanced on the speeder, holding Lune by the hand. He stepped carefully onto the wall, helping Lune to stand beside him. They balanced there, waiting, while Solace cut back on the engines.

She expertly guided the craft to nudge against the wall. Astri's face was white with suspense.

Lune and Trever stepped easily into the craft and were pulled into seats by Astri's eager hands.

"Get to the base. I'll join you," Ferus shouted over the wind to Solace.

He watched as the ship zoomed away. Then he

turned, jumped into the borrowed speeder, and raced back up to the roof. He picked his way past the blasted beams and took the stairs down to street level to meet Darth Vader.

CHAPTER NINETEEN

The dark side was so strong that Ferus felt like he was being engulfed by it as he walked up to Vader. He had to pull himself together and act as normal as he could, not like he'd just fought a heated battle.

"I think we're tracking the same person," he told Vader. "Any luck?"

Vader didn't answer for a moment. A long moment. Ferus tried not to sweat. All he could hear was the tunnel-echo whooshing of Vader's electronic breath-mask.

"Several battalions of droids and troopers have been demolished. Prowler droids as well. The saboteur has help."

"Lucky that you came prepared," Ferus said, indicating the armed activity around him.

"Strange. Captain Chainly reported that lightsabers were involved."

"That doesn't seem likely," Ferus said, relieved that he'd hidden his own.

Vader didn't answer. "Do you have the saboteur's name?"

"Quintus Farel," Ferus answered.

"That is an alias."

"That's all I have. The apartment was empty when I got there."

"You took a long time to find me."

"I was searching. I thought we should work together."

"I work alone."

He could not have bested Darth Vader in battle. Ferus knew that. But he had won this round simply by walking out the door. For some reason, he had the protection of the Emperor. As long as he had that, Vader couldn't touch him.

Vader didn't have to speak. Ferus knew he was angry. He could feel how difficult it was for Vader to suppress it. Behind his words was fury and frustration. He had gotten to him just by standing here, just by existing. . . .

Something tickled Ferus's memory. Something familiar about this scene. What was it? He felt there was something here that he should be able to grasp but couldn't.

"Lord Vader?" Vader's comlink crackled. "Space cruiser seen leaving the area, sir."

"Go after it!" Vader commanded.

"Too late for pursuit, sir. I sent a patrol ship after it."

"Send everything you have."

Vader switched off the comlink. "It does not matter," he said. "They cannot leave the planet."

The helmet turned back toward Ferus. The blank eyes seemed to study him. Then Vader turned and walked off, his cape swirling behind him.

CHAPTER TWENTY

Keets and Curran sat on the floor together in the holding room.

"What's taking Sauro so long?" Keets asked.

"I don't know," Curran said. "But the longer we're here, the better. Once we get into an Imperial detention center, we're sunk."

"You mean we're not sunk now?"

The door hissed open. Zackery stood there, a reluctant look on his face. "Senate regulations say I have to send in food."

Keets brightened. "Things are looking up."

A cook droid wheeled in. "Things are done by the book in the Senate, young man," she advised Zackery.

"Don't call me young man!" Zackery shouted at her.

"Sorry, old man!" the droid trilled.

Zackery snorted and stamped out, but left the

door ajar. He stood, his hand on his blaster, and watched.

Keets looked at the droid closely. Despite the fresh paint job, he recognized the antique droid WA-7. It was the same droid that had worked in Dexter's Diner. She'd served him sliders and the slop Dex called a drink at least a hundred times.

Yes, things were definitely looking up.

She placed a tray on the floor next to them. A large pot of liquid, two mugs, and two veg turnovers. She took the items off the tray and then took the tray away again. "Enjoy!" she said.

She began to wheel out. Keets reached for the cups.

"I'm not thirsty," Curran said.

"Oh, you'll like this." As soon as WA-7 was between them and Zackery, Keets took the small blaster out of the pot.

Curran's reaction time was excellent for a once-bookish senatorial aide. He jumped to his feet and charged as Keets moved forward with the blaster. At the same moment, WA-7 threw the heavy metal tray at Zackery's neck. It hit him hard, and he staggered backward. Keets flipped the blaster and used the hilt to knock him on the head. Zackery fell heavily.

Keets turned to the three security droids and blasted them into smoking metal.

Keets and Curran stepped over Zackery's inert body. They peered out into the hallway. The Senate was coming to life again as Senators, aides, and droids reported for work. Intent on their business, no one gave them a second glance. Together with WA-7, they moved into the stream of workers.

"I suggest a fast exit," WA-7 said. "I can find my own way out. Say hello to Dex for me!"

She wheeled away. Keets and Curran knew the Senate building as well as the homes they'd grown up in. Within moments, they had found the closest exit. They were free.

CHAPTER TWENTY-ONE

Solace steered Astri's star cruiser straight into the hold. They all climbed out and made their way to the cockpit.

"So far so good," Oryon muttered. "No Imperial guards rushing the ship."

"Contact the dockmaster and get clearance," Solace said. "That will be the real test. I'll start the departure checks."

They all stayed in the cockpit, too anxious to find seating. Astri kept Lune close by her side.

"Request permission to take off," Oryon spoke into the comm unit.

"Checking data," the dockmaster replied.

Minutes ticked by.

They exchanged worried glances.

"It's taking too long," Solace said.

* * *

"Of course they changed the registry numbers!" Sauro screamed at the Imperial officer sitting at the databank that monitored all Imperial traffic. "Look for a ship that matches its description."

The officer keyed in more data. He sent another holographic space map into the air.

"Now give me the data from every spaceport near its last known position," Sauro said, pacing behind him.

"Senator, there is a ship on the landing platform on Samaria. . . ."

Sauro stopped pacing. Samaria! Of course. The hijacking hadn't been random at all. They'd gone straight to the planet where Ferus Olin was. How could he have missed it? He'd been so blind.

"That's it. Get me the dockmaster, now."

"The spaceport is still in the hands of the Samarians, sir, not us —"

"Just get him!"

A moment later, an obviously nervous dockmaster was on the comm.

"Yes, there is an Imperial ship. It's a diplomatic ship. It's been cleared for departure."

"Stop that ship! Now!" Sauro shouted.

"But sir, it's an *Imperial* ship," the dockmaster said patiently. "You must have misunderstood me. All Imperial ships are cleared to —"

"Listen to me." Sauro leaned toward the comm. "Revoke the order and stop that ship or I will personally escort you to an Imperial prison for the rest of your life."

"Ah, sir, I'm sorry. But I'm afraid the clearance has already been granted. The ship just cleared Samarian airspace. Sir."

Sauro slammed his hand down on the console, breaking two sensors.

His assistant hovered by his elbow. "Sir," he whispered. "The Emperor would like to see you. Now."

CHAPTER TWENTY-TWO

Darth Vader left the mess of the botched pursuit behind and climbed into his custom-made airspeeder. He sat for a moment as his driver waited for orders.

Ferus Olin. So insignificant that Vader had forgotten about him. He had been a blip in his past. Something that had happened long ago, a small jealousy that had never blossomed into a real, mature hatred. He would have been happy never to have seen him again.

But of course he survived the Clone Wars. He hadn't been a Jedi.

Vader didn't think of him as a rival. He had never even achieved the status of a Jedi. He had left as a Padawan. A student. Ferus couldn't come close to matching his power.

But why was he here? Why had his Master employed him at all?

There could be only one answer. Ferus could be

one of the few left in the galaxy capable of becoming a Sith apprentice. Capable of being trained, capable of rising to the heights of power.

Of course it was laughable to think this could be the case. But perhaps his Master didn't think it so laughable.

Vader was still hampered by the incredible injuries he'd endured. He could never have the full power the Emperor had. It was the unspoken thing between them. The thing he could never change.

Vader let his artificial hands relax before they clenched.

No, Ferus was not a serious threat. But he had won anyway, had he not? The saboteur had escaped. Ferus had aided in that escape. Of that he had no doubt.

Had there been another lightsaber? Had Ferus found another Jedi?

The old jealousy surged in him, the old envy.

He didn't try to dismiss it. Now he knew how to use it.

The deeply enjoyable part of his conversion to the dark side of the Force was this feeling of sureness. The dark side eliminated doubt.

He never wanted to live with doubt again.

He never wanted to be reminded of what he'd been.

He nodded to his driver, who pushed the speeder

engines and lifted the craft into the air. He would control this situation. Sauro was not the problem now.

Ferus Olin was.

Ferus stood concealed behind one of the columns of the spaceport and watched as the Imperial ship took off from the landing platform in Sath. He had to be sure his friends were safe.

What now?

He turned his face toward the city. Astri had managed to tell him how to solve the problem with the BRT droid computer. If Larker gave the okay, the city could be back to normal as early as tomorrow morning, the changes made to protect those fighting the Empire.

He was anxious to return to the secret base. Anxious to see the progress Raina and Toma had made, anxious to see how Garen was faring. And it was hard to say good-bye to Roan. It would have been good to ride through the atmospheric storm to get to the asteroid. Good to be with friends. To rest, even for just a day.

But something was telling him not to leave. Things had changed. He had taken on a job for the Emperor. He was now working for the Empire, at least on the surface. He was certain that Palpatine didn't trust him, but that wouldn't prevent him from becoming a double agent.

He was certain that Palpatine would have another job for him, and soon. They were both aware of the game they were playing.

He would risk it.

Risk it, and learn what he could. He'd enter the heart of the darkness he hated and feared.

He would need all his strength, he knew, to survive it.